Burning Man

4/29/204

For Scott —
Pleasure working with you —
Every good wish for your writing —

E

Also by Edward Falco

NOVELS
Saint John of the Five Boroughs
Wolf Point
Winter in Florida

STORIES
Sabbath Night in the Church of the Piranha
Acid
Plato at Scratch Daniel's

SHORT FICTION
In the Park of Culture

NEW MEDIA
Chemical Landscapes, Digital Tales
Circa 1967–1968
Self-Portrait as Child w/Father
Charmin' Cleary
A Dream with Demons
Sea Island

PLAYS
The Center
Possum Dreams
The Pact
Radon
Sabbath Night in the Church of the Piranha

Burning Man

STORIES

Edward Falco

SOUTHERN METHODIST UNIVERSITY PRESS
Dallas

This collection of stories is a work of fiction. Names, characters, places, and incidents are either the product of the author's imagination or are used fictitiously.

Copyright © 2011 by Edward Falco
First edition, 2011
All rights reserved

Requests for permission to reproduce material from this work should be sent to:
> Rights and Permissions
> Southern Methodist University Press
> PO Box 750415
> Dallas, Texas 75275-0415

Cover photo: "Burning Man" by Aaron Logan
Jacket and text design: Tom Dawson

Library of Congress Cataloging-in-Publication Data
Falco, Edward.
  Burning man / Edward Falco. — 1st ed.
      p. cm.
  ISBN 978-0-87074-568-3 (alk. paper)
  I. Title.
  PS3556.A367B87 2011
  813'.54—dc22

                                             2010044431

Printed in the United States of America on acid-free paper
10 9 8 7 6 5 4 3 2 1

For Judy Bauer

Contents

Among the Tootalonians | 1

Wild Girls | 25

Little America | 47

Smothered Mate | 63

Burning Man | 71

Candy | 99

Winter Storms | 121

Mythmakers | 147

American Martyrs | 163

Jekyll Island | 185

The Athlete | 199

Acknowledgments

Most of the short stories in Burning Man were previously published: "Among the Tootalonians" in *The Gettysburg Review*, "Wild Girls" in *The Missouri Review*, "Little America" in *Southwest Review*, "Smothered Mate" in *Notre Dame Review* and *Masters of Technique: An Anthology of Chess Fiction*, "Burning Man" and "Winter Storms" in *Playboy*, "Candy" in *Five Points*, and "Mythmakers" in *Shenandoah*.

The author would like to thank the National Endowment for the Arts and the Virginia Commission for the Arts for their support; and the Corporation of Yaddo and the Virginia Center for the Creative Arts for the gift of time, space, and encouragement.

Among the Tootalonians

VAL'S MARRIAGE WAS DEAD, HIS CAREER WAS STALLED, AND his hair looked like shit. As if that wasn't enough, the outer world, the other world, the world of cities beyond the city where he lived, of children who were still children, unlike his own who had grown and left him years ago, that other surrounding world that came to him daily through television and computer images, in newsprint and slick magazine type and broadcast voices, that other world was descending once again into chaos and madness, the same chaos and madness unchanged it seemed since the beginning of time, only now the buildings that were falling were bigger, as were the numbers of people easily accessible for slaughter. Thus no one had time to worry about Val. No one called, although he was living entirely alone for the first time in his life, in the West, which was as foreign to him as the plains of Mars, in Boise, Idaho, for God's sake. No one had time to call. Not his two daughters from his first marriage, Evelyn and Barb, both of whom still lived in the beleaguered East, in the target city of New York, New York. Not the son from his second marriage, Jordan, who had his own drug disaster going that overshadowed even the current world disaster. And certainly not his third and most recent ex, who had dragged him to Boise in the first place and then left him, but not for a younger man, which would have made too much sense given that Val was her senior by twenty-six years, but for an even older man, a man of seventy plus years, a man some dozen years older than Val and not even as well-off, an artist of some kind, a sculptor who taught at the local university, a wizened, rickety creature who hung out at a local coffee shop where he was held in some kind of western art reverence by the Idaho intelligentsia.

Val was not in a good place. He was not a happy man. The house where he lived echoed around him like the interior of an abandoned mall. He had moved to Boise because Bess, his ex, had been offered a good position at the same university where her current artist-lover reigned. She had selected the house. It was on the outskirts of Boise, with a view of burnt-out foothills sloping off into an endlessly browning distance. For reasons he could never grasp, she loved the vast, treeless openness of the view, which she considered a great find for a house so close to the city. He hadn't argued. She was a still young woman with an active academic career, and if that career took her west, to Idaho, to a house with a view of burnt-out foothills, what choice did he have if he wanted to be with her—and he did want to be with her—than to follow? The requirements of his own career were indeterminate since he wasn't sure he had a career any longer. He seemed to be retired. He had been a historian, an author of books on the Civil War, the first of which, published when he was thirty-five, had earned him enough money—thanks largely to a TV miniseries—to live comfortably for decades; the next of which, after earning him another decades-sustaining advance, had sold miserably and been reviewed worse; and the last two of which were still residing quietly on the hard drives of his various computers. After those

Among the Tootalonians

two full-length books that had taken a combined eleven years to write, after all that effort and energy and time invested in projects no one felt were valuable enough even to merit publication, after all that he didn't have the heart to start again, to immerse himself one more time in one more project editors and publishers would shrug off with attitudes ranging from annoyance to disdain. Plus, in his heart, deep in his gut, he knew he'd rather rot in hell than ever have to deal with his agent again. And the only thing worse than dealing with his agent would be trying to find another one. So he found himself without work, with no idea what he was supposed to do, alone in Boise, where he knew no one other than Bess, a woman who had left him for a man who could be her grandfather, in a time when the world was a frightening and dangerous place where shadowy enemies were blowing up buildings and poisoning the air and food, and people were doing their bestial best to kill and maim and spread terror and agony—and it was under those circumstances that he had gone downtown earlier in the day to have his hair dyed. He told the girl assigned to him, a seventeen-year-old, still in high school, to color it light brown, a shade he hadn't seen in the more than ten years since his hair had turned completely gray. Nonetheless, when she was done, it looked a hell of a lot more blond than it did brown.

 The decision to dye his hair had been pretty much spontaneous, though he had never liked being gray. In his fifties the gray annoyed him terribly because he felt it changed people's attitudes toward him in subtle ways. It was as if others suddenly assumed he was a person who could no longer have potential in his life, that there could no longer be possibilities available to him, that suddenly he had to be at the end of his journey, either accomplished or failed, and he balked at that assumption, unwilling to give up his own image of himself as someone still searching, in his life and in his art, for new perceptions and new possibilities. Now, however, at age sixty-two, he had adjusted to the gray, to people's shifting attitudes toward him, as he had adjusted in general to the facts of advancing age. People always made dumb assumptions about others based on appearances. It was nothing he couldn't deal with. And so it was with a sense of surprise and slight unreality that he found himself sitting in a heavily padded chair facing a full-length mirror, talking to the image of seventeen-year-old Tiki, explaining that he wanted his hair dyed light brown, and pulling an old snapshot of himself out of his shirt pocket.

Tiki, who was standing behind him looking him over in the mirror, ran her spread fingers through his hair, pulling it out from the sides of his head. She gazed at it for a long moment, with the look and attitude of a professional. When she said, "This is going to make you look twenty years younger," Val couldn't keep himself from smiling like a thirteen-year-old boy who'd just been told he looked sexy. He closed his eyes and leaned back in Tiki's chair and tried to ignore the sting of chemicals as she set to work. Even before she was done, however, long before she clicked off the blow-dryer and offered him the hand mirror so he could appraise the back of his head, he clearly saw the full extent of the disaster. It was hard to articulate just how utterly wrong this particular shade of color looked with his particular face. All the creases and wrinkles etched by sixty-two years of life suddenly seemed garish and shocking as a field of scars. A countenance that had forty-five minutes earlier appeared authoritative now looked ridiculous. It wasn't just that the hair color didn't go well with his skin color, that it, somehow, gave his skin a slightly greenish hue; it was that the haircut she had given him along with the coloring egregiously aggravated the color problems. The girl obviously had little or no experience cutting men's hair. She had cut it so short that his ears, which stuck out slightly, were absurdly accentuated, and she had trimmed the hair over his forehead in a near straight line, giving him a sort of demented medieval look. Val stared a long time in silence at the wondrously strange image looking back at him.

Tiki said, "It looks kind of more blond than I thought."

"You think?" Val said.

She added, "We could like, you know, try to make it darker."

Val leaned back in the chair and gripped the armrests as he appraised himself thoughtfully in the mirror. "My wife left me for this really old guy," he said. "He's an artist. J. Jackson Wellington?"

"Oh, I've heard of him," Tiki said. "He's pretty famous. He's like in the newspaper a lot."

"He has a show opening downtown tonight. A retrospective."

"That's right," Tiki said. "That's what I was thinking. There's an article just in the paper today. It's at that new gallery, Western Spaces or something."

"I'm invited," Val said. "I haven't been out in a while. I thought I might go."

"Oh," Tiki said, and she looked at his reflection again, worriedly. "You sure you don't want to try to go a little darker?"

Val considered the offer. He thought he probably should wait while she once again applied the chemicals and worked in the dye, and he probably should put up with the sting and the long awkward minutes while the smelly gunk did its work and strangers traipsed in and out of the salon. Instead, he heard himself say, "No thanks, Tiki. What do I owe you?"

•••

By the time Val's taxi dropped him off outside Western Spaces, the brief but intense thunderstorm that had dropped an inch of rain on the city in less than an hour had long ago sailed far beyond the clustered humanity of Boise and off into the surrounding desert, so when Val stepped out of the cab and into a puddle that covered his foot up to the ankle, he was surprised and he wasn't surprised. He thought, *Where the hell'd this puddle come from?* and then, *Of course.*

The cabdriver, who looked like he couldn't possibly be old enough to have a driver's license, slid toward the window. "You okay?" he said, lifting himself up, trying to get a look.

"It's nothing." Val shook his leg and stamped his foot on the street.

"Oh, hell," the cabbie said, once he realized what had happened. "I'm very sorry, sir. Sir, I guess—I didn't see it, sir. Sir, is there anything I can do?"

Val said, "You can quit calling me sir."

The driver backed away from the window. He appeared hurt.

"Look," Val said. "It's nothing. It's okay." He counted out the fare and placed it in the young man's hand, adding a five-dollar tip to prove he was sincere.

Once the cab had disappeared around a corner, he sat down on a streetside bench and took off his shoe and sock. He was wearing his best summer suit, a light brown, eighteen-hundred-dollar garment, along with a dark shirt and matching dark tie that had cost him more than he used to pay for rent back in the days before that first successful book-publishing deal. He dried his shoe as best he could with his handkerchief and wrung out his silk sock before trying to shake it dry. Down the street, a pair of bright red double doors opened, and a half-dozen people stepped out onto the sidewalk accompanied by the sounds of laughter and talking. They held wineglasses aloft, carried plates of food, and were all dressed neatly but casually. One guy was wearing jeans and a white shirt with one of those western string ties Val had never seen anyone wear in the real world, only in movies and on television. He removed the invitation from the inside pocket of his suit jacket. As he feared, several lines down from Bess's neatly handwritten *Let's not be enemies* were the crisply printed words *Casual Dress*. Val spread his arms out along the back of the bench and looked up at the moon, which was so huge and bright it seemed as though it might have fallen out of its orbit and dropped a few miles closer to the earth. He put the invitation back in his pocket, pulled on his wet sock and soaked shoe, tying the lace securely in a bow, and started toward the gallery and the partyers on the street. In his peripheral vision, he could see his reflection accompanying him in a long plate-glass window. Even without turning to look, he saw with a surprising degree of clarity that the brown suit he had chosen emphasized the new and still deepening blondness of his hair, so that it looked like a shock of flame arising from the wick of his neck above the dark candle of his body.

 Once off the street and past the sidewalk wine drinkers and inside the gallery, he found himself comfortably obscure in the midst of a crowd of milling, mostly young to middle-aged people, though here and there were individuals and couples his age and older. What had he expected? That the crowd would fall back aghast, cover their mouths with one hand and point with the other at his hair? Actually—as he expected would happen or else he wouldn't have ventured into the room—no one even noticed him. Or if they did, they weren't being obvious about it. They continued with their conversations, which seemed mostly to be about bombs and war and biochemical attacks, while they sipped wine and ate hors d'oeuvres and moved from sculpture to sculpture or stood firmly planted in a comfortable group. To Val's dismay, he found himself deeply impressed by Wellington's sculptures. He had hoped to find giant silver eagles or bronzed Indian maidens, but instead he was surrounded by contemporary figures constructed out of bits and pieces of computer parts, as well as gears and ratchets and rusted tools and a thousand other things you might find in a mechanic's garage or an old barn. The success of the pieces was not in the conceit but in the particulars of each construction, which seemed to speak simultaneously to the dehumanization of man and his irrepressible humanity. In some of them it was almost impossible to say where that spark of humanity was coming from, given how completely the figures were constructed of cogs and gears, computer chips and transistor boards. It was as if, somehow, there was a yearning human soul trapped within and looking out from these figures constructed from the inhuman stuff of our industrial-technological culture. After looking at only a few of the works, Val felt a deep, deep depression wrapping itself around him like a quilt. He could feel himself growing heavier.

"This is just such amazing shit, isn't it? Don't you think? It's just so, oh my God—"

Val braced himself against the weight of a woman who was leaning on him as she spoke, as if she might fall to the ground in a faint without his support.

"It's just so completely overwhelming, I could slit my wrists just— Oh my God," she said again, and then covered her mouth with both hands and rested her head on Val's shoulder.

Val glanced around the room. He didn't know exactly why he

was looking, but it seemed possible this person might have attendants searching for her. She was a slight woman who appeared to be in her late thirties to early forties, wearing white boots, black leather pants, and a red silk blouse with the top three buttons open so that the most common movements left her small breasts momentarily exposed to view. Her hair was bright blonde with about two inches of black roots accented by the way she wore it pulled back, which was a current fashion, Val understood, and looked good on her, though he couldn't say the same for the gold eyebrow ring or the small silver stud on the tip of her tongue.

"They're just so . . . eaten up," she said, and then pulled herself away from Val and looked him in the eyes for the first time. "I know you see it," she said, with an air of reprimand. "You looked like you were going to completely collapse a moment ago. My heart went out to you, really. I see it too. We're simpatico. We can talk." She made a sweeping gesture with her hand, indicating the scores of others chatting under the track lighting or shuffling over the bright hardwood floor, moving from sculpture to sculpture. "These others, they're all tootalonians."

Though he was curious, Val decided not to ask her what she was talking about. Instead he asked politely, "Do we know each other? Have we ever met?"

"Oh. Please don't disappoint me," she said.

"I'll try not to," he said.

"We've always known each other." She sounded as if she was annoyed at having to answer his question but willing to do it for him, to get it out of the way. "We've known each other since the beginning of time." She turned to the sculpture again. "Look at this," she said, gesturing toward the distorted bust on a pedestal at eye level in front of them. "This is us in our world right now. Is it a man or a woman? It doesn't matter. It's completely misshapen and warped by its fight against the radio waves and television signals that are trying to control it, trying to make it into a monster instead of a human being. I know you see that," she said. "I can see that you see it."

Val said, "You give me too much credit." He looked around the room again and noticed that though he was alone with this woman with no one within ten feet of him, there were dozens of people clustered around every other sculpture in the gallery. He said, "That was just jealousy you saw."

"What was?"

"My reaction. I was just jealous. That's what you saw. Crushing jealousy."

The woman seemed to consider this for a moment. She put her hands on her hips and looked him over. "No," she said, finally, as if satisfied and certain in her determination. "No, that's not it," she said. "You may have been jealous of Wellington's talent, but what really got to you was his depiction of our universal, slow, cultural mass death, how we come into this world so beautiful only to be destroyed little by little, year by year, no matter how hard we struggle, till there's so little left of the beautiful that it's like this—" She gestured toward the bust. "Peeking out, buried, desperate not to die."

Val said, "You think so?"

"Look at what's happening right now," she said. "Did you know they poisoned the city? Did you hear that on the news tonight? How can we stay beautiful? How can we not hate them when they're trying to kill us so horribly, burning and crushing and poisoning our neighbors, our children? How can our hearts not turn into the hearts of monsters? You tell me."

Val said, "They poisoned the city? Boise?"

"Read the papers," she said, dismissing his question. She pointed at the bust again. "You know the only way it can not die, what me and you see peeking out from behind that almost-monster's eyes?"

"No," Val said. "How?"

"There is no way," she said, and looked meaningfully at him. "It has to die. That's the way it is. It's just looking for someone who can touch it so it can touch someone in return. And then that someone's not just someone anymore, and they're together. That makes it better. Maybe that even makes it worthwhile."

"Really," Val said. He thought he understood what she was talking about, which frightened him slightly, so he was immensely pleased when he saw Bess emerge from behind a crowd of people and cross the no-man's-land that surrounded him and the crazy woman. She was beautiful in a simple black dress, with her hair up, a plain gold necklace accentuating her still youthful skin. "Bess," he said, and he was surprised to find himself taking an excited step toward her, a burst of energy at the sight of her pushing him forward.

"Val," she said, and then addressed the woman. "This is a family emergency," she said. "Please excuse us just one moment."

"My ex-wife," Val said to the woman as Bess pulled him away through the chatter and laughter, past the perfumed and cologned bodies, away from the narrowing eyes of the woman in her black leather pants and silk blouse, and toward the red doors and the street.

Once outside, she said, furiously, "Do you know that woman? Is she with you?"

"Why?" Val said. He was taken aback by her anger.

"Why? She's nuts, that's why. She's insulted half the people in the gallery. Are you telling me she's with you?"

"Calm down," Val said. "I've never seen her before. You don't know who she is?"

"No one knows who she is. What's she talking to you about? What's she saying?"

"Well . . ." He scratched behind his ear and looked off down the empty street while trying to find some coherent summary of their conversation. "Well," he said again. "I think basically she's been telling me how much she admires your— What do you call J? Lover? Significant other?"

"I'd guess she admires J," Bess said, sarcastic. "She offered him oral sex right in front of me."

"She what?"

"I want to call the police, but J's like—" Bess sighed. "J's like the prototypical hippie: everything's cool, no problem."

"She just came up to the both of you and offered—"

"It was rhetorical," Bess said. "She was, in her own insanely crude way, trying to tell him how much she liked his work."

"Oh," Val said, and laughed. "What did she say? She just walks up to the two of you and goes *J, you're such a great artist I'd like to—*"

"You think that's funny?" Bess put her hands on her hips and squared off in front of him. It was a posture Val had seen many times before.

"Look," he said. "I don't know the woman."

"You never saw her before tonight?"

"Never. Total stranger."

"Well how come she's talking to you like you're old friends?"

"I don't know," Val said. "She says we're simpatico."

This time Bess laughed.

"What's that mean?" Val said. He crossed his arms over his chest and leaned in toward her, which was a posture Bess undoubtedly also understood.

"All right, listen," she said. She looked up at the moon, which was almost directly overhead. "Moon's unbelievable tonight, isn't it?"

"It's incredible," he said. "We should be bringing in the harvest."

Bess said, "I apologize for being so angry with you, especially since it's been so long since we even talked." She touched his arm.

"That's all right," Val said. "How are you?"

"Wonderful," she said. "I'm wonderful." She smiled, and her eyes were bright and untroubled for a moment. "I'm happy."

"Okay." Val nodded, his lips pressed together tightly. "I'm happy for you then."

"Thank you," she said. "Look. Val. Can I ask you a huge favor?"

"What? What can I do?"

"Could you find a way to get her out of here, please? She seems to like you. Maybe you could just . . ."

"What?" he said. "You want me to take her home with me?"

"I didn't say that. Take her for a cup of coffee. There's an all-night diner a couple of blocks from here."

"Oh, come on, Bess." He turned and looked away from her. "I don't want to have coffee with this woman."

Bess stepped in front of him and took his arm in her hands. "Please, Val. As a favor. I put so much time into this opening, and she's ruining the whole thing."

"Why? What's she doing?"

"What's she doing? She's insulting people. She's being rude. She keeps calling people tootalonians."

"What's a tootalonian?"

"How the hell would I know what a tootalonian is?" Bess said, letting go of his arm. "The woman's mad!"

"Bess..." Val took a few slow steps away from her, back toward the gallery. As he did so, the guy with the western string tie stepped through the doors tapping a cigarette out of its red cardboard box. Directly behind him came an attractive older woman carrying two full wineglasses. "Excuse me, buddy," Val said. "Do you mind if I hit you up for a cigarette?"

The man looked askance at Val and seemed on the verge of telling him to go to hell before he noticed Bess standing rooted in place with her arms folded, watching them. He nodded to Bess, gave Val a cigarette, lit it for him, and then walked away several yards with the wineglass woman following him like a butler delivering his drinks.

"That's Harris Wills," Bess said as Val joined her again, taking a long drag off his bummed cigarette. "When did you start smoking again?"

"Just now," he said. "Who's Harris Wills?"

"Rich guy. Look. I've got to get back inside. You don't have to— I mean I wouldn't have even asked. It's just—"

"I'll give it a shot," he said. "As a favor to you. Let me finish this cigarette."

"Thank you, Val." She touched his hand and hesitated, looking as if she was torn between getting back to the gallery and staying another moment.

"Yes?" Val asked, squinting his eyes a little, comically. "Something else?"

Bess pressed her palms together in prayer position, fingertips touching her chin. She said, "This is out of respect and affection I tell you this, Val. But your hair looks just completely ridiculous. Really. You need to know. My God, who gave you that cut? Did they use garden shears? Who did the color, a grade-schooler with a yellow crayon? It's just outrageously— You look— You look— Absurd."

Val said, "You think so?"

"For heaven's sake, Val. Everyone's talking about it in there."

"Everyone's talking about it? Everyone's talking about my hair?"

"Between you and the nutcase, this opening's turning out to be Boise's gossip event of the year."

Val ran his fingers through his hair. "You don't think it makes me look youthful and suave?" he said, his tone dead serious.

Bess was clearly confused by his response, and then angered. "Did you hear me?" she said. "It looks terrible. I didn't even know it was you when I first saw— I thought, who's that wacko? You look pathetic, Val. You look like an old man stupid enough to think blond hair will make him look young. It's embarrassing to me. You're my ex, for Christ's sake. You reflect on me." She yanked the lapel of his jacket. "And didn't you see the *casual dress* on the invitation? Are you *trying* to make me look bad?"

"I don't know what to tell you," Val said. "I'm sorry, but I think the hair makes me look twenty years younger. I think it looks terrific."

Bess looked him in the eyes a long moment, and then turned without a word and went back into the gallery. Up the block, Val noticed Harris Wills and his companion sipping wine and watching him as if he were on stage in the midst of a performance.

He half expected applause as the scene ended with Bess's exit. He hesitated a moment longer on the street, where he stood entranced in a kind of stunned euphoria. He felt weightless and giddy, the world around him as inconsequential as a dream. He couldn't care less what Harris Wills or Bess or anyone else thought of him. He found it all amusing: the scene, the moment, the people, the situation. He wished he had a mirror so he could look at his hair. The hell with them all. The more outrageous it looked, the better.

"Excuse me. Harris." He stopped on the way back into the gallery and crushed his cigarette into the pavement under his still-wet shoe. "Have you heard anything about someone poisoning Boise or anything like that?" When Harris didn't answer, but only looked back at him, shoulder to shoulder with his woman friend, Val moved in front of him. "It's just, someone was saying something about poisoning Boise, and, I thought— I mean, I don't know whether she's a nut or what."

Harris said, softly, "There appears to be evidence that someone may have tried to dust the city with toxic chemicals."

Val said, "That's true? When did— I haven't heard a thing."

"Breaking news."

"So, what? Are we in danger? I mean, should we—"

"No," Harris said. "It's unlikely we're in any danger. The city engineers are finding trace amounts of toxins spread throughout Boise, not enough to do any damage; but since these are not naturally occurring elements, the theory is that someone might have tried to poison the whole city."

"That's just—" Val said. "Is there not going to be any end to all this?"

"I wouldn't worry about it," Harris said. "If someone did try to poison the city, it didn't work. Keep in mind there's two documented cases of terrorists crop-dusting Tokyo with anthrax and not managing to give anybody as much as a cold."

Alongside him, Harris's companion clutched her wineglass to her chest. "Terrorists crop-dusted Tokyo with anthrax?"

"Twice," he said. "That we know of."

"This world," she said, and turned to look again at Val. "It's a sin."

Harris said to Val. "Are you a friend of Bess's?"

"She's my ex," Val said. "We were married eight years."

The woman said, "She was married to you?"

"Eight years," Val answered.

Harris nodded. His companion watched Val, wide-eyed.

Val muttered to himself as he turned his back on the couple. "Poisoning Boise, Idaho . . ."

Inside the gallery, he found the woman alone in a corner, staring forlornly at one of Wellington's pieces, a standing figure arrested at the moment of stepping back from something, fear palpable in every line and angle. "Hey," he said, moving in front of her, blocking her view of the figure. "What's your name?"

"Alice," she said. She sounded downright depressed compared to the enthusiasm of their earlier conversation.

"Well, listen, Alice," Val said. "Let's get out of here."

"Want to go back to my place?" she asked, perking up. "I live right across the street."

"Really? You live right here?"

"Plus," she said, "I've got some kick-ass grass."

"Amen," Val said. He offered her his arm, which she took with a smile.

On the way out, he turned to look for Bess and found that

half the gallery was watching. In a far corner, seated side by side in a pair of black straight-back chairs like reigning monarchs, Bess and J were also watching. Two very young women, probably J's students, knelt beside his throne, and a handsome, long-haired boy in blue jeans and a white cardigan held one of Bess's hands in both of his. They were all transfixed, and for a moment Val considered bowing with an extravagant flourish before turning to leave. Instead he only laughed slightly, amusedly, and exited the gallery with Alice on his arm.

Outside, Harris and his companion had disappeared. Alice said, "She never loved you, you know. I could see that instantly. You were just somebody to make her life better, just as Wellington is." She let go of Val's arm and maneuvered in front of him. "Older men," she said. "You see a young woman, and you're all— You'll do anything. Suddenly you're all fools."

Val said, "She thought I was somebody I turned out not to be."

"Say again?"

"It's not her fault," he said. "She's not a gold digger, a career advancer. It wasn't like that."

"Oh my God," Alice said. "You're still crazy for her. That's so damn sad. I'm so sorry. Honestly."

"It's just—" Val said. "Look. Did you say you lived across the street?"

Alice turned and pointed directly across the street at a two-story brick building, the bottom floor of which appeared to be an antiques shop.

"When you say across the street," Val said, "you mean across the street."

"I'm like that. So? Do you want to?" She pointed to her building.

"Yes," Val said. "Surely."

As they crossed the street on their way to an alley that led around behind Alice's building to a flight of wooden stairs, Val noticed a white Cadillac parked midway back in the alley, two wheels on the street and two on the sidewalk, a pair of empty wineglasses side by side on the dash. He imagined Harris and his companion scrunched down in the backseat, hoping not to be noticed, and he made a point of walking close to the car, brushing his leg against the back door as he passed. Climbing the stairs, he asked Alice what a tootalonian was.

"Word I made up," she said.

"Really? What's it mean?"

"Did they tell you I was crazy?" she asked. "Because I'm not." At the top of the stairs, she lifted an empty flowerpot from the railing, found a bright metal key, and unlocked her door. "I'm different," she said. "I'll grant them that. But not crazy. They're the ones that are crazy." She put the key back under the flowerpot, then grasped and turned the knob with her back to the door, looking at Val. "They're the ones who're crazy," she repeated. "They're the ones."

"Okay," Val said. "I believe you. So what's a tootalonian?"

"I was at a party," she said hurriedly, clearly not much interested in the explanation, "and this guy was off in a corner tooting coke all by himself, and it came to me: tootalonian. That's what they are. All they care about's themselves. See?" she said. "I told you. I'm not crazy." She pushed the door open and gestured for Val to enter.

Before she came in behind him and turned on the light, he noticed several glowing red points punctuating the darkness in a far room. He knew immediately they were sticks of burning incense, since the odor was thick enough to choke on. At first he didn't recognize the smell, but when she turned on the light, and he saw two Persian cats sitting on the sink counter amid what looked like a month's worth of unwashed dishes, he pinned down the smell as a pungent mix of cat shit and incense. "Mind if I open a window?" he asked. "The odor's kind of intense."

"Hi kitties," she said, addressing the cats, who looked back at her imperiously. She closed the door and went directly to a kitchen drawer, which she pulled open and began rummaging through. "No," she said to Val without looking up from her search. "Go ahead. I don't mind."

In the darkened bedroom, which appeared to be the only other room in the apartment, Val walked over piles of clothes and garbage covering the floor and went directly to the incense sticks. He yanked each of them out of their holders, pulled open the window, and dropped them into a half-inch-deep puddle of black rainwater collected on a wide, tar-papered ledge. Across the street, in the gallery, which he could see into through a line of high windows, Bess stood in the center of the room and clapped her hands. She appeared to be calling the gallery to attention. Val watched her with interest, but turned around when the lights went out behind him.

In the moment or two he had to take in his surroundings while gathering up the incense, he had noticed that the walls were covered with newspaper clippings. There wasn't enough light to make out what the clippings were about, but it was clear there were scores of them, all fastened to the walls with silvery duct tape, giving the room the appearance of a stereotypical serial-killer's hideout, the place the cops always find near the end of the movie, just before the climactic rescue. When he turned away from the window and looked back again into the darkened bedroom, he saw Alice moving from place to place igniting one candle after the other by pulling the trigger of a red rifle-shaped lighter. After she was done and the room glowed in the flickering light of a dozen burning candles, she cleared her bed of clutter, sat down on a mattress covered with a red silk sheet, and began to undress. Val sat back against the open window ledge and watched her, at first amused by how brazenly she was pulling off her clothes, unzipping and kicking off her boots, undoing the hook and zipper of her leather pants before casually unfastening the small, clear buttons at the sleeves of her blouse, yanking it out of her pants and opening the center buttons, and then taking it off with a shrug of her shoulders and tossing it onto the floor. But once her stomach was exposed, Val's amusement disappeared. A lightning-bolt scar descended from just below the right side of her rib cage across her belly down almost to her navel. It was wide and jagged and ugly, not the kind of scar modern surgery might produce. When she stood up to take off her pants and her eyes met his for a moment, he had to look away. He noticed again the clippings taped to the wall and saw for the first time that many were very small, some only a few lines of newsprint, and he realized there may have been hundreds of them. In the candlelight he could see repeated in the headlines the words *assault, battery, rape, murder.* He looked again at Alice and saw that she had turned away from him in the process of stepping out of her pants. Across her bare back in a diagonal line running from her left shoulder to her waist was a series of three oblong scars that pointed to yet another similar scar on her buttock and two more on the back of her thigh. A queasy roiling started in the pit of his stomach. Around the edges of the scars, her light skin darkened and reddened. He guessed, from the look of them, the wounds were very old. As he stared, the roiling in his stomach progressed to nausea and he had to turn away.

As he looked out the window, he heard the mattress squeak followed by the crinkling of paper, and he imagined that she was sitting up on the bed, perhaps watching him as she went about rolling a joint. Across the street, Bess and J stood in the center of the gallery, surrounded by a crowd that appeared incredibly young and immensely beautiful, flawless in the moment of celebration. Bess held up a wineglass as she spoke, and the crowd raised their glasses back to her. With his head out the window, breathing in the night air, Val's sickness subsided. His forehead and upper lip were wet with a patina of sweat brought on by the nausea, and he cupped a handful of rainwater in his palms and brought it to his face. In his hands, he saw his own reflection and was filled for a moment with an overwhelming tenderness toward the image looking back at him, as if he were some kind of aging, modern Narcissus, only it wasn't his own beauty he loved, but the lack of it. And it wasn't love. It was tenderness toward the lined and creased face, the thinning, ridiculous hair, the dark circles under the ruined eyes. As the image spilled through his fingers, leaking back into a disturbed picture of the moon looming over ragged lines of buildings, he lifted it to his lips, as if in a kiss, and washed his face with the cool, dark water.

Behind him, he heard paper rustling, but when he turned to look, instead of finding Alice rolling a joint, he found her sitting up on the red silk sheets, her legs crossed under her, reading the local newspaper. She seemed utterly comfortable, utterly nonchalant, as if she regularly read the newspaper naked in bed while a stranger watched. "Alice?" he said, approaching her. "What do you think of my hair?"

"What about it?" she asked, looking carefully up at him for a moment before losing interest. She threw the newspaper over the side of the bed and then looked down after it. "It's heartbreaking, isn't it?" she said. "What's happening? How the world is?"

Val touched her leg. "Turn over," he said. "I'll give you a massage."

"Oooh," she said, throwing herself onto her belly and stretching her arms out across the mattress. "A massage."

Val knelt over her thighs and touched her back softly at first, gently kneading the flesh of her neck and shoulders, before, encouraged by her sighs of pleasure, he pressed harder, absorbed in his efforts, working the skin of her back, massaging the wounds, while her sighs grew into deep moans that rose to the ceiling and circled about the room before wafting through the window and out into the moonlight over a poisoned world.

Wild Girls

When Deborah said, "Jason, you know I'm a little in love with you," he pretended not to hear. Deborah was twenty-one. She was a tattooed and bejeweled art student currently taking his painting class. He had met Marilyn, a graduate student with whom he had become friends over the past few years, for a drink at a noisy East Village bar, a bar, it turned out, that Deborah frequented. When she saw him sitting in a high-backed booth with Marilyn, whom she knew, she came over to say hello. Marilyn invited her to join them, and now the three of them had been drinking and telling stories for hours. Jason looked away, across the bar, where he could see their booth reflected in a tall mirror. On a good day in bad light he could pass for a guy in his mid-forties. He worked out daily and was in better shape than many of his twenty- and thirty-year-old students, who were given at this stage in their lives to smoking, drinking, and a generally dissolute life. His life, on the other hand, was compulsively ordered: he woke, ate breakfast, and went directly to his studio to paint all morning. When he was finished painting, he exercised for an hour to an hour and a half, which included a two-mile power walk. Then home to shower before teaching his late-afternoon and evening classes. He had followed variations on that routine most of his adult life. For the past three years, since the breakup of his last serious, long-term relationship, he had followed the routine exactly. His productivity in that time had skyrocketed, and his art career had jumped to a higher gear—but he also had begun to think of himself as a kind of monk, since he had no social life whatsoever anymore beyond an occasional evening out—like this one—for drinks with one of his students or an old friend.

In the tall mirror, he saw two young women staring at each other while a middle-aged man looked away, across the barroom. Both women, were surrounded by the resonant aura of their youth. Their skin was alive with it. The air around them vibrated with it. Deborah had a tattoo of a snake curling over her bare shoulder and along her collarbone to her neck, where its small red eyes watched whomever she faced. Marilyn, who was about ten years older than Deborah, looked nonetheless like a high school girl in comparison. She wore jeans and a man's undershirt with a V-neck that showed cleavage and a quarter-size tattoo of a rose high on her right breast. Deborah's dark hair was long and silky and streaked bright red. Marilyn's hair was naturally blonde and cut boyishly short. Deborah wore a slinky black halter top that left her midriff bare above white pants cut impossibly low. Marilyn's jeans were tight, but cut like a man's, with a high waist. They were both beautiful. And he, blessedly, didn't look so bad himself in his ordinary blue jeans and a black short-sleeved shirt that showed off muscular arms. His hair was graying and thinning, but it was still there, a respectable head of it looking silvery against the black of his shirt.

Marilyn placed her elbows on the table, folded her hands together, rested her chin on her knuckles, and leaned across the table to Deborah. "Jason," she stage-whispered, "appears to be pretending he didn't hear you."

"Do you think?" she said, her eyes going wide, playacting great surprise. She pushed Jason's shoulder. "Jason," she said, "are you pretending you didn't just hear me tell you that I'm kind of in love with you?"

Jason watched the three of them a moment longer in the tall mirror. Deborah had a mischievously wicked look about her, clear even across the room, reflected in a smoky mirror. Marilyn, watching Deborah, looked amused. "How much have you had to drink?" Jason asked. He nudged Deborah's knee with his own as he turned back to her with an exaggerated look of reprimand and touched the rim of her martini glass, out of which she had emptied three or four bright red cocktails of some kind. "What are these potions you've been drinking?"

"I'm not drunk," she said, folding her arms across her chest as if indignant. "My tongue hath been loosened, yes," she said, "but I'm not drunk."

Marilyn said, "I'm not drunk. I've only had three watered-down bourbons." She paused dramatically and smiled as if something juicy was about to be revealed. "And I'm," she said, "also a little in love with you."

"Really?" Deborah spun around to face Marilyn. Her expression was somewhere between pissed off and shocked.

Jason finished off the last of his scotch. "I think we've all been drinking too much," he said, "and it's getting late."

Marilyn said, "It's only ten o'clock, Jason. This is when I usually start getting dressed to go out for the night."

"Well, see?" he said. "There you go. By ten o'clock, I'm usually in my pjs, sipping a nice hot cup of decaffeinated tea, getting ready for bed."

Both girls laughed at that, assuming, he guessed, that he was putting them on. He wasn't. His tone was exaggerated for effect, but the facts were gospel. By ten o'clock, most nights, he was curled up in bed with a cup of tea on the nightstand, reading a book or a journal.

Deborah leaned across the table to Marilyn, her chin resting in the palm of her hand. "Are you really that into him, too?"

"Yes," she said, "I am." She winked at Jason. "He's cute, don't you think? I go for big, muscular types—but they have to be brainy or talented too."

Deborah looked at Jason appraisingly. "It's not his looks so much," she said to Marilyn, though still gazing at Jason. "I think it's because he's so fucking decent," she said. "I'm dying to corrupt him."

Marilyn said, "He does have that decent thing going."

"Jesus," Deborah said, as if suddenly exasperated. "I've been throwing myself at him all semester, and he acts like he doesn't notice. Then he just goes on being . . . decent. It's maddening. I want to throw him down and fuck his brains out."

"Deborah," Jason said, the reprimand in his voice serious now. "Really . . ."

"I think it's because he's an accomplished artist," Marilyn said, ignoring Jason entirely. "How many men are we going to meet in our lives with Jason's kind of talent? Think about it. Before we go back to the little towns we came from, surrounded by little lives."

Deborah raised her eyebrows at Marilyn. "I'm from San Francisco," she said. She looked pointedly at Jason. "And I plan on being just as successful and accomplished as Jason here, if not more so."

"Good for you," Jason said.

"I'm from Coldwell, West Virginia," Marilyn said. "God help me."

"Coldwell, West Virginia," Deborah repeated. "That sounds . . . hard."

"Trust me," Marilyn said. "I'm not going to meet anyone like Jason there."

Jason said, "May I say something?"

Deborah said to Marilyn, "What do you think? Should we let him join in the conversation?"

Marilyn said, "Why not?"

Both girls gazed at him and then said, "yes?" almost simultaneously.

At the front of the bar, a noisy collection of young couples pushed through the door in midconversation, laughing and shouting at each other as they came in off the street. Everyone in the bar stopped for a moment and looked at them, and then the group fell silent when they realized they were the center of attention. For an eerie few seconds, the only sound in the bar was a plaintive saxophone solo, one Jason had heard before, moody and evocative, filled with sensual grief, but barely audible over the sustained hum of air-conditioning. The air smelled thickly of smoke tinged with a hint of perfume. Then, as quickly as the silence had descended, it lifted and the bar was filled again with noise and activity. It was getting crowded as the evening wore on. People were two deep at the bar and standing around talking in clumps everywhere.

"Just," Jason said, "I'm afraid it really is getting late for me." He held up his empty glass. "It's getting to be time."

"Jason," Marilyn said, leaning across the table and grasping his hand, "I refuse to let you go. You always run away when we get to this point in the evening."

"And what point is that?"

"The point when something might happen."

Deborah said, "He does that with you too?" She shoved Jason. "That's just what you do with me!"

Jason removed his hand from Marilyn's. "I think you're confusing *running away* with *leaving*. I've never *run away* after seeing either one of you. I've *left*, and gone home. Which is just . . . what else?" He shrugged, suggesting he was nonplussed by the notion that he would do anything other than leave and go home after having spent time with either of them for whatever reason.

Marilyn said, "We've been flirting for years now. Don't pretend you're not aware of it."

"Me too," Deborah said. "You flirt with me too, Jason." Under the table, she touched his foot with hers.

Jason could come up with no immediate reply and so was silent as he returned Marilyn's stare. It was true that he flirted with both of them. He always flirted a little with women. It meant nothing. "I suppose I flirt," he said, at first serious. Then he tried to make a joke of it. He ran his fingers through his thinning hair. "I'm getting old fast," he said. "I'm on the steep downward slope to the grave. I crave the attention of beautiful young women—means I'm not quite dead yet."

"Oh, stop," Deborah said. She nudged his leg under the table. "You're not so old."

"Yes he is," Marilyn said. "He's fifty-five." She touched Jason's hand. "But I don't think that's what it's about, the way you are with women."

"You don't?"

"I think you're lonely and full of desire," she said. "You look at women as if you'd like to swallow us whole, as if you'd like to lick every inch of us, from our toes to the top of our heads."

Deborah laughed and put a hand on Jason's shoulder. "I think Marilyn might be projecting just a little bit there," she said.

Marilyn laughed too. "I might be," she agreed. "But I do think the lonely and desire stuff works, don't you? Isn't that what you see in his eyes?"

Deborah dropped her hand from Jason's shoulder to his forearm. Her eyes met Marilyn's and they both smiled sly smiles. "Jason," Deborah said. "You came of age in the sixties. I bet you've engaged in an orgy or two in your time."

Jason covered his face with both hands and rested his elbows on the table, as if he needed to take a little nap. He had, in fact, in his early twenties, when he would have called himself a hippie, participated in a sexual adventure involving more than two people—but that was before he turned his back on the self-indulgence of the times. He remembered the encounter as a strange mix of comedy and lust. He knew Marilyn and Deborah both thought he was wrestling with temptation—but he was actually wrestling with something more like annoyance. It bothered him suddenly that these two girls felt so free to toy with him. They both knew he wouldn't take them up on their offer—even if he were seriously tempted—if for no other reason than the knowledge of how his colleagues would eviscerate him once the story got out, as it inevitably would. Marilyn's precious analysis of him as lonely and full of desire was especially annoying. The glibness of it stung. He felt, suddenly, like an adult who had let two precocious children get the better of him.

"Ah," Deborah said. She patted Jason on the back of the head. "Look what we've done to the poor guy."

"We're seductresses," Marilyn said, apparently to Deborah. She touched Jason's elbow. She whispered, "We're just too wicked."

Jason lifted his head from his self-imposed darkness. Amid the growing clamor of the barroom, the various shouts and loud laughing and squeals, he heard himself say to Deborah, "I have a king-size bed in my apartment. It's only a couple of blocks from here."

Deborah's face went blank for a moment, and her mouth opened slightly. "Oh my God," she said. "Really?"

Marilyn watched Jason intently for a few seconds before she got up from the table and said, "I've got the check. Meet you guys out front."

For an apartment that had cost him close to a million more than ten years earlier, the lobby, such as it was, looked remarkably dilapidated. A glass door set in a plate-glass wall opened onto a small room with mailboxes and a second door that led to the elevator. Jason unlocked the outside door, held it open for the girls, and then pulled it closed until he heard the familiar click it made when it locked. For a moment, he stood with his back to Deborah and Marilyn, looking out at the street, at a line of worn-down buildings and at the hunched-over figure of an old man shuffling along the sidewalk. When he turned around, the girls were standing side by side, holding hands, watching him. The red streaks in Deborah's hair, the snake tattoo on her neck, the halter top that left half her breasts exposed and the pants cut so low she surely had to wax to wear them—all of that did nothing to keep her from looking like a worried little girl. Marilyn, in comparison, looked confident and greatly entertained by the situation. "Cute," he said, nodding toward their clasped-together hands.

"You're cute," Marilyn said. "You should see how scared you look."

"I look scared?" he said, unlocking the second door. "Why would I be scared?"

"Beats us," Marilyn said, as if fully empowered to speak for Deborah.

Jason held the door open for them and gestured with a flourish to the elevator. Deborah entered the room first. "I'm not scared," Jason said, and as Marilyn walked past him, he ran his hand from the small of her back down over her ass. He smiled when she flinched.

Once the three of them were in the elevator, he inserted the key in its slot and turned it sharply. The small compartment lurched once before smoothly beginning its slow ascent.

"This is cool," Deborah said. "You have your own elevator." She appeared to be trying to hook her thumbs in the pockets of her jeans, but the pants were much too tight and her hands kept falling awkwardly across her thighs.

"So is this something you've done before?" Jason asked. He looked back and forth from Marilyn to Deborah.

"I don't think you ever answered that question yourself," Marilyn said. "Have you? Ever done anything like this before?"

"Very long time ago," Jason said, "in a distant galaxy . . ."

Deborah laughed and Marilyn said, "How long ago? Twenty years? Thirty years—"

"Thirty years!" Deborah said, as if that span of time was inconceivable.

"More than thirty, actually—"

"Oh my God," Deborah said, and pushed him. "You are old!"

Marilyn said, "Tell us the story."

When the elevator door opened onto his living room, both girls seemed surprised. Marilyn did a quick scan of the room, her eyes raking over the bookcases, the wall-mounted plasma TV, the high ceilings, the various artworks, sculptures and paintings, the hardwood floor and the spare furnishings: a sectional couch, a leather recliner under a black lamp, end tables and a long table in front of the couch that looked like a work of art more than a coffee table. "Wow," she said. "Gorgeous place."

"Is that an original Andy Warhol?" Deborah asked, walking into the room with her eyes fixed on a prized Warhol print.

"That's a complicated question with his work," Jason said, joining her in admiring the screenprint, "but, essentially, yes. It was a gift from him."

As if she found it barely possible to believe, she said, "You knew Andy Warhol?"

Jason didn't answer for a second. He did some quick calculating and figured out Deborah must have been about two years old when Andy died. He realized that to her Andy Warhol—someone he had known quite well, someone with whom he had spent a great deal of time, a kind of teacher as well as a friend—to her Andy Warhol was a historical figure, someone she had studied in art history classes, as distant to her as Hieronymus Bosch. He laughed off her amazement. "He died not even twenty years ago," he said. "Wine?" he called across the room to Marilyn. He started for the kitchen and his wine cabinet.

"Not me," Marilyn answered. "I think we should get right to the threesome." She leaned against the wall and called to Deborah. "This is a Cindy Sherman." She pointed to a photograph alongside her head. "Jason was her *teacher*."

"Briefly," Jason said. "And not in photography, obviously." He flopped down on the couch. "So," he said. "Are we having class here, or what?"

"Don't get petulant," Marilyn said.

Deborah said, "I'll have that wine. I'm losing my buzz."

Marilyn said, "I'll get it." To Jason she said, "Is it in the kitchen?"

"Cabinet, next to the sink."

Once Marilyn disappeared into the kitchen, Deborah, who had been studying the Warhol, took a few steps back from it, turned in a slow circle taking in the room, and smiled when her eyes lighted on Jason. She seemed surprised to find him there, watching her. "I want a place like this one day," she said softly, almost reverently, "full of art, full of all the famous artists I've known."

Jason, without intending to, made a little sound, something like a laugh, that could have been interpreted as disdainful.

Deborah didn't notice. She sat alongside him and put her hand on his knee. "You really do think I have the talent, don't you, Jason? It's not just encouragement?"

"Absolutely," he said. He put his hand over her hand, which was resting on her knee. "You have all the talent you need."

From the kitchen, Marilyn called, "Hey! You guys aren't starting without me, are you?"

"No way!" Deborah called back. She smiled radiantly at Jason and then jumped up and kissed him on the cheek, a friendly peck. "I definitely need some more wine though! Can you believe we're doing this? Oh my God!"

"Hardly," Jason said. When he could think of nothing else to say, he let himself stare. The way she was draped over the couch, with her legs tucked under her and one arm flung over the backrest, she might have been posing for a magazine ad. The lines of her bare stomach were exquisite, and he was tempted to reach across the space between them to touch her hair, which was lustrous and long and would feel lovely, he knew, sliding through his fingers.

"Yes?" she said, watching him. "What are you thinking?"

"Nothing," he said. "I was just thinking about touching your hair."

"Do you like my hair?" She grabbed a strand and hung on to it. "I need that wine, first," she said, and she pressed both hands over her stomach. "I'm getting butterflies! I've never done this kind of thing before! What's it like?" She pushed him. "You're all up for it, aren't you?" she said. "And here I thought you were like this totally controlled guy!"

"He's in control," Marilyn said. She came in from the kitchen carrying an open bottle of wine and three glasses.

"What did you pick?" Jason asked.

"An Italian," she said, holding up the bottle for him to see. "Nothing too special." She looked at the label. "2003."

"Good choice," he said, helping her with the glasses.

"Fill me up!" Deborah snatched a glass and held it out to Marilyn. "This is so fucking crazy," she said. "Can you believe we're doing this?"

"Sure I can," Marilyn said. She leaned over Jason to fill Deborah's glass. "It's going to be an . . . experience," she said. "It's going to be something we'll never forget."

"I'll bet," Deborah said, and she downed half the glass of wine in two swallows.

"You are nervous," Jason said.

"Top me off." Deborah held out the glass again. "I need to get my buzz back."

"You need to relax," Marilyn said, refilling her glass. "We don't want you drunk, honey," she added, with an exaggeratedly serious look, as if she might have been a mother giving a daughter worldly advice before a big date.

"I just need a little more of a buzz," Deborah said to Marilyn. To Jason she said, "So you've done this before? You didn't tell us. Did you like it? Was it great?"

"Yes," Marilyn said, "tell us." She slid closer to Jason on the couch, and rubbed his ankle with her foot, encouraging him to talk.

Jason sighed, and then quickly ran through the details. "I was in my early twenties," he said. "I kicked around Europe a while after school, and I met this woman, her name was Livia, in, believe it or not, the British Museum Library. We were both looking at art books. Anyway, we got to be friends. She invited me back to her apartment. It was, like, midafternoon—and . . . we went to bed. Then, in the midst of things, this other woman walks in, and, it's like— Livia jumps up, I'm in bed naked— Turns out, the woman is her lover. She's gay. Or, bi, I guess. And, we're like, busted. So, this other woman, she's: okay, fine. She looks me over, takes off her clothes, and— The three of us spent the rest of the afternoon together. That was it. Never saw either of them again."

"How crazy is that?" Deborah said. "That's such an artist's story, don't you think?" She looked across Jason to Marilyn. "Bet that kind of thing wouldn't happen in Coldwell, West Virginia."

Marilyn said, theatrically, "Actually . . ."

"Oh my God!" Deborah shouted. "You had a threesome in Coldwell, West Virginia?"

"Actually," Marilyn repeated, "several."

"Several?" Jason said. "As in three? Four?"

"A lot more than that," she said. "It was a fairly regular event."

"Oh my God," Deborah said. "What do you mean, *regular*?"

"My ex . . . ," she said, and then shrugged, as if even she couldn't explain her own behavior. "I was a very different person then, and, my ex, he'd bring home girlfriends all the time— I was just expected . . ."

Jason said, "But were you into it? Was it something you wanted?"

"Not really," she said. "It's hard to explain. He wanted it, and, it was just, like . . . The person I was at the time . . . I don't know, I felt like I had no choice. It's hard to explain, really. I just, did what he wanted me to do."

"Oh my God," Deborah said, "that's so, like, fucked-up."

"Yes," Marilyn said. "Completely." She raised her eyebrows and made a face that suggested she too was amazed at how fucked-up she had once been. She added, "It just took me a while to figure it out."

Jason asked, "How old were you when this was going on?"

"Young," Marilyn said. "Very young." She winked at Deborah. "Younger than our young friend here."

"Damn," Deborah said, "you guys have so much . . . history."

"Everybody has history," Marilyn said.

"Not me," Deborah answered. "I've been in school my whole life. You guys have been married and done all that real-world—" She stopped abruptly and reddened a little, as if she was embarrassed. "Shit," she said. "I don't think I know what I'm talking about." She laughed, and then finished off her wine with Marilyn and Jason watching her. After a long moment of silence, she said, "Well don't just both stare at me!" She was probably trying to be amusing, but she sounded peeved.

"You know what?" Marilyn said. She smiled at Deborah and then ran her fingers through Jason's hair. "I think Deb and

I should go get ourselves ready in the bedroom." She reached across Jason, leaning her body over his as she put her wineglass down on the table, and took Deborah's glass away from her. "You," she said to Jason, her voice dripping with sexual suggestiveness, "should wait out on the deck." She got up, took Deborah by the hand, and pulled her up from couch.

"Whoa," Deborah said, as if getting up had made her dizzy. She laughed and leaned against Marilyn, who wrapped her arm around her waist. "I guess . . . ," she said, and laughed again. "Here we go!"

"Here we go," Marilyn echoed. She kissed Deborah on the cheek and winked at Jason. "Leave the door open so you can hear us," she said. "We'll call you when we're ready."

"Oh my God," Deborah said to Jason. "This is so crazy." She looked at Marilyn and said, "I think I'm getting excited."

At that, Marilyn kissed her gently on the lips and said, "This is going to be fun."

To Jason she said, "That way?" She looked across the apartment to a dark hallway.

Jason nodded, and then she waved him out to the deck before turning around, taking Deborah with her, and heading down the hallway to the bedroom.

After both girls had disappeared into the master bedroom, and the light had come on, casting its precise yellow rectangle into the hallway and halfway up the wall, Jason listened for a while on the couch as drawers opened and closed and the sliding door to his walk-in closet squealed slightly as it was pulled along its track, stuck briefly, and then squealed again until, fully opened, it banged against the wall. Then the mattress squeaked and both girls laughed, and Jason's thoughts were pulled, disastrously, to his first wife and the son they had adopted once they learned Jason couldn't father children. The boy's name was Calin. They had adopted him from Romania as a toddler. He was a smiling, beatific, robust angel of a boy whom his wife had fallen instantly in love with, as had Jason. They spent a month in Romania working out the adoption, and then six more wonderful months with Calin at home before he got sick. Then a year and a half of misery before it was all over, everything all over, Calin gone, Teresa, his wife, back home with her parents. She didn't even bother with the details of a divorce. She just picked up and left a few days after the funeral, leaving Jason to contact lawyers. During those six months at home with Teresa and Calin, which Jason still thought of as the best six months of his life, the boy loved to jump on the mattress. Jason would stand on one side of the bed and Teresa on the other. They'd hold his hands while he jumped and squealed.

Jason took the wine bottle with him out onto the deck, where he poured himself a glass as he looked out blankly across the hazy air to a line of apartments over street-level shops. In a window directly across from him, a young woman walked through her kitchen dressed in a white T-shirt and black underwear. It took her a second to cross the room and then she was gone, leaving Jason feeling as though he were surrounded by sexy women. Everywhere he looked there were women, one more alluring than the next. He took his wineglass and stretched out on a lounge chair. To his left, he could see into his apartment, all the way back to the yellow light from his bedroom. To his right, tall apartment buildings rose all around him. Though he knew in a moment Marilyn would call his name and he'd go to his bedroom to find her and Deborah awaiting him, it still seemed impossible. It all felt more like a game than a sexual intrigue, and though he supposed in a very short while he'd be in bed with Deborah and Marilyn doing the things one does in such a situation, it still didn't seem real. Marilyn seemed more amused than aroused, and Deborah seemed like a child. He had told her, honestly, she had all the talent she needed to succeed as an artist. What he didn't tell her was how incredibly unlikely it was she'd have the luck and resolve she'd also need, along with the even more unlikely chance she'd have the kind of vision as an artist that was of interest to anyone other than herself. Or that she'd have the kind of character and intelligence that could translate the chaos of experience into something meaningful and resonant, or, even better and more rare, something beautiful. Those were the miracles she'd need. Talent was plentiful.

At the sound of footsteps, Jason turned to find Marilyn walking toward him along the hallway. She was wearing his white terrycloth robe, which was absurdly big on her and all the more sexy for the way she had it rolled up and tucked in. When she saw he had noticed her, she stopped and waved him into the room.

"Problem," she said, softly.

"Really?" Jason picked up the wine bottle and his glass and joined her in the hallway, stopping to close the big glass door behind him, muting the sounds of traffic and the hum of a helicopter passing nearby.

"She's freaking," Marilyn whispered. "She's scared—and she's embarrassed because she's scared. She wants to . . . but she feels like she's going to throw up . . . Et cetera, et cetera."

Jason couldn't repress a broad smile. "I wonder what happened to all the bravura from the bar?" he asked. "Did you remind her that it was her suggestion?"

"I did," Marilyn said. "Believe me, she's fully aware. I think that's why she's so embarrassed."

"We'll have to let her off the hook," Jason said.

"Really?" Marilyn said. She looked disappointed.

"I wouldn't want to corrupt her," he said, alluding to Deborah's remark at the bar about wanting to corrupt him.

Marilyn smiled at that. "She's so beautiful," she said. "The tail of that snake tattoo wraps around her breast . . . Jesus, you could die she's so deliciously ripe."

Jason broke into another broad smile that built to a small laugh. "It's *her* you're into," he said. "I'm such an egoistical ass. I thought it was me."

She put her arms around his neck and kissed him on the cheek. "I do like you," she said. "You're sweet. All those threesomes with my ex, though . . . They had an unintended consequence."

"You figured out men were expendable."

She smiled. "He liked to watch," she said, still whispering. "For a long time, he had to push me. Then, I got to like it."

"You're wild," Jason said. "You're something else."

"Hey!" Deborah's voice came loud from the bedroom. "Are you guys talking about me? I hear you whispering!"

In the bedroom, they found Deborah sitting up on the left side of the bed, a pillow folded behind her back, her legs stretched out and crossed at the ankles. She was wearing one of Jason's shirts that came down to mid-thigh. She looked as though she had primped and propped herself up to look as sexy as possible. The light blue shirt was unbuttoned far enough to show the body of the snake descending from her collarbone and beginning to wrap around her breast. The bottom of the shirt fell open between her thighs accenting the valley of tanned skin where her legs met. "I've got it together now," she said, with a coyness that suggested she was amused at herself, at the unexplainable childishness of her behavior. "I think it was just a little momentary panic."

"Well, very good," Marilyn said. She was standing beside the bed, and she shrugged off her robe and let it slide to the floor, revealing her body with obvious pride.

Deborah looked across the bed to Marilyn, and at first the coy and sexy expression on her face held, but then, a second later, it seemed frozen there unnaturally, and a second after that her eyes welled up with tears and she covered her face with her hands and sobbed, "Oh God. I can't, I can't. I'm so embarrassed!"

"Jesus Christ," Marilyn said. She put her robe back on.

"I'm so humiliated," Deborah said.

"Do you fucking believe this?" Marilyn said to Jason. She sat on the right side of the bed and stretched out her legs.

"Don't be mad," Deborah whimpered, still hiding behind her hands. "Please . . ."

"I'm not mad," Jason said. To Marilyn, he said, "You're not really mad, are you?"

Marilyn seemed to have to think about that for a second. "No," she said, finally. "I'm not mad."

Deborah peeked out from behind her hands. "Really?"

"Really," Marilyn said.

Jason left the bedroom to get the wine and the glasses, and when he came back he found the two girls sitting where he had left them, Marilyn looking at one of his early assemblages hanging on the right side of the room, and Deborah looking at the pulled curtains on the left side of the room. He handed them both wineglasses, filled them, then filled his own glass before turning out the lights and pulling back the curtains, letting the city lights from the street and the surrounding apartment buildings illuminate the room. He took off his shoes and socks and climbed into his bed between them, facing them, sitting up with his back against the footboard.

"It's not quite an orgy," Marilyn said, holding out her wineglass for a toast, "but it's nice."

Jason clinked glasses with Marilyn. Deborah, though, continued staring out the window.

"Deborah," Jason said, "everything's fine. Really."

"Are you sure?" she said, still looking out the window. She swiped a hand across her eyes, wiping away tears. "I feel like such an idiot. And it was my idea to begin with."

"You're not an idiot," Marilyn said. "You're just confused, which, who isn't at twenty-one?"

At that, Deborah turned to look at them. She said, solemnly, "You guys really aren't mad at me?"

Marilyn said, "I swear I'm not mad." She laid her bare ankle over Jason's bare ankle. "And Jason here," she said, "I bet this is the hottest night he's had in ages."

"Unquestionably," Jason said, and took a sip of his wine.

"You guys are sweet," she said, but she still sounded sad. She followed Marilyn's lead and laid her bare ankle over Jason's other bare ankle. She smiled wanly, as if she was deeply disappointed with herself, as if she had just discovered she wasn't the person she thought she was and she couldn't quite get over it. She turned again to look out the window, her eyes wet with tears, her body slumping with her sadness.

Marilyn looked as though she wanted to say something to Deborah. She watched her a moment, her eyes full of tenderness, and then turned wearily to look in the direction of the assemblage and the wall. She seemed suddenly very tired as she held the wineglass to her chest and disappeared into herself.

With both girls looking away, lost in their own worlds, Jason was free to stare at them unabashedly. He let his gaze move slowly over each of them, taking in the subtle shifts in skin tone where the curves of their bodies were shadowed or illuminated by the dim light from the window. He followed the deep green of Deborah's snake, with its pinpoints of red for eyes, until it disappeared under the soft blue of her shirt, the shirt's thin cotton fabric shaping itself to her breasts. On the inside of Marilyn's leg, the faint darker line of a vein traveled up her thigh widening before it was lost under the white nap of the terrycloth robe. He watched them so intently he could feel himself dropping into one of those moments when time and experience and history and knowledge and ideas—when everything slips away and all that remains is vision, all that's left is the act of seeing. When he was filled with that moment, when the room seemed to hum with the absence and fullness of it, he lay his head back on the footboard and turned his eyes blankly to the ceiling. As if from someplace outside himself, he saw the three of them in his bed, each looking in a different direction. He closed his eyes and let himself feel the place where their bodies touched, their skin over his skin at his ankles. In his body, he felt the touch vividly. In his mind, he entertained the idea of them, the idea of the three of them at three different stages in their lives, come together in this instant. When, in his heart, he felt a bubbling up of gratitude, he tried to breathe more slowly. If he could have, he would have stopped breathing entirely, anything to extend the moment before it passed, as it would, and the world returned with a rush like the explosion when someone touches a match to a torch, like the blaze when the torch goes up in flame.

Little America

TECHNICALLY, VIVIAN WAS LOOKING AT ME AS SHE GROPED around under the passenger seat, but really her head just happened to be pointed in my direction, her right cheek smashed against the glove compartment. We were driving through Wyoming. I smiled at her. She said, "Where the hell could that damn thing have gotten to?" This was my first time crossing the country by car—well, by van—and I was stunned by the emptiness of the terrain. Hours and hours of driving surrounded by the same ugly barren rock and dirt as far as I could see. Vivian was a West-head. The West this, the West that, the West was God's splendid paradise on Earth. She had lived in Montana all her life before her job transferred her to Manhattan, which is where we met. Myself, I had never been out of New York. For me, upstate New York was untamed wilderness. Wyoming was . . . I don't know. It was another planet or something.

Vivian said, "What are you looking at, Jeeves?" My name is Anthony, but Vivian had taken to calling me Jeeves because I insisted on doing all the driving. Jeeves was her name for all chauffeurs. "Never mind," she said when I didn't answer quickly enough. "I can see what you're looking at."

I was looking at her breasts, of course. She had on a lightweight summer dress cut low and loose, and the way she was bent over, it would have taken a saint not to stare. When I reached down to touch the objects of my gaze, Vivian pulled away, sat up straight, crossed her arms over her chest, and gave me one of her withering stares.

"Uh, oh," I said. "Bad touch?"

"Very good, Jeeves."

In the two years we'd been together, Vivian had been working hard to teach me the difference between good touch and bad touch. Good touch was romantic and sexual, and it happened when she wanted to be touched, when she gave me the right signals. Bad touch was, like, if she was preparing dinner and I happened to notice her ass as she stood with her back to me and I put my hand there. That was bad touch. It usually resulted in the withering stare. Problem was, it wasn't always so damn obvious. And Lord help me if I didn't touch her when she wanted to be touched. That meant I didn't love her. I sighed. "I didn't realize you didn't want to be touched," I said. "Forgive me."

"You didn't realize?" She looked at me as if I had to be an idiot. Then she sighed.

As a couple, we tended to sigh a lot.

"Forgive me," I repeated. "But this was planned as a romantic trip, remember? I mean, the plan was, romance."

"Sure it was," Vivian said. "That was the only way I could get you out of Manhattan."

"Oh? So it was a deception? The promise of sex was a subterfuge to get me out of Manhattan?"

"Right. It was a deception, Anthony. I didn't really want to have sex with you on this trip. In fact, I got a yeast infection so I wouldn't have to—even though I spent the whole year planning this stupid vacation."

I saw her point. My aggressive attitude dissolved.

"Anthony," Vivian said, "why are you such an asshole?"

"I'm sorry, Vivian. Forgive me for touching my fiancée when I notice her breasts. Forgive me for thinking she might actually want to be touched."

As a couple, in addition to sighing a lot, we also tended to drop into sarcasm pretty readily.

"I'm scrunched up against the dashboard looking for the cap to a tube of vaginal cream," she said, "and you thought I might want to be touched? What is wrong with you, Jeeves?"

"There's nothing wrong with me," I said. Then added, "What's wrong with you?"

Vivian reached into the litter bag at her feet and pulled out the tube of cream with the missing cap, which was less a tube and more a perverse cross between a tube, a syringe, and a push-up pop. She pulled back the plunger and held the device dangling from her fingertips. "Do you know what I had to do with this thing, Jeeves?"

"I can make a guess."

"That's right," Vivian said. "Exactly."

"And so?" I said. "Is it my fault?"

"Yes. It is. It's your fault, Jeeves."

"It's my fault?"

"Yes."

I pondered this. How was it my fault that Vivian had a yeast infection? Because of work and trips and scheduling, we hadn't had sex in weeks. For a moment I was nonplussed. Then my training came back to me. When she got unreasonable in an argument—she had explained this to me many times—it meant she was feeling vulnerable and needed to be reassured. She recommended gentle, loving touch and kind words. I reached across the

49

seat and held her hand. "Vivian," I said. "I love you very much. I think you're beautiful."

She was silent a moment. Outside, the same relentlessly barren landscape sailed by unending. "Sure," she said, subdued. "Now, when I'm twenty-five, you think I'm beautiful. What are you going to think when I'm fifty-five and look like a stereotypical Italian grandmother?"

"Are you worrying about the wedding?" The wedding was planned for Labor Day weekend. It was still a couple of months away.

"I'm not," she said.

"Then what are you worrying about?"

"I'm worrying about how I'll look when I'm fifty-five."

Vivian was small, barely five-foot, with big breasts and a stocky body. She derided it as a weightlifter's body. I liked her looks. I liked her body. I liked her body a lot. Still, as she had told me often, it was not the body she would have chosen had someone thought to ask her. I said, "I find you very attractive, Vivian."

"Oh," she said. "*Attractive.*"

"*Beautiful,*" I said. "I said *beautiful* first."

"And when I'm fifty-five?"

"When you're fifty-five, I'll be sixty."

"So?" Suddenly she was angry again. "Mr. Sickkens—was there ever a more perfect name?—Sickkens just turned sixty."

Mr. Sickkens was her boss. He'd recently left his wife of twenty-plus years to marry the company CEO, who was only thirty-something. "Sickkens doesn't look sixty." I said. "No way."

"You won't look your age either!" Now she was yelling. "Men never do!"

"But I will," I said. "I promise. I promise to age gracelessly. By the time I'm sixty, I'll look like shit. I swear."

"You promise?" She seemed placated. I detected the hint of a smile.

"Absolutely." I pulled her close to me and put my arm around her. She kissed me on the cheek.

For the next several minutes, we drove on like that, in silence, harmoniously. Outside the car, the scenery floated past, impossibly unchanging. I was amazed. I found it hard to believe America still had such huge, empty places. I had flown over the country many times. From the air, you just see this big flat space that turns into mountains for a while, and then you're in Los Angeles. Amazing how different it was on the ground. Hour after hour after hour of driving and nothing but rubble and white rocks and barren ground as far as you can see, no matter where you look. It was beginning to make me seriously anxious. I wanted to complain about the landscape again, but I knew better. Vivian had a proprietary attitude toward the West, and every time I complained, which I had been doing with some frequency the past two days, she took it as a personal insult.

But I couldn't keep myself from commenting. I tried not to sound negative. "It's just . . . stunning," I said. "The emptiness of it."

Vivian sighed. "It's not empty," she said. "It's just not overdeveloped, like the entire East Coast."

"Not overdeveloped? Isn't that a bit of an understatement?"

"Don't start," Vivian said. "It's not empty. It's capacious."

"Capacious," I repeated, hoping she'd tell me what the word meant before I had to admit not knowing. Actually, not remembering. *Capacious* was one of those reading words, words that turn up in writing but hardly ever in real speech. Like *lugubrious*, or *effluvium*. I could recall having read it and looked it up before, but I couldn't recall what it meant. Vivian had used it only because it was one of last week's words-of-the-day, which, itself, was a mystery to me—the whole word-a-day thing. Vivian's vocabulary was excellent, but, suddenly—this started like a week after I proposed to her—she has to improve her vocabulary. Every day's a new word, which she gets out of a vocabulary book she hauls around. This morning's word had been *cinereous*, which means *consisting of or resembling ashes, a gray color tinged with black*. All morning it was *Look at that cinereous cloud*, and *Look at that cinereous patch of ground*. Once she even used it metaphorically, claiming she was in a cinereous mood. I advised her against that one. I had some authority in the area since I had been an English major at Colgate, and I was a writer for *The Today Show*.

"That's right," Vivian said. "Capacious."

"Okay. I can't remember what it means. Tell me."

"Roomy," Vivian said, happily. "Spacious. Large enough to contain great quantities of things."

"That's right," I said. "I knew but I forgot."

"Right," she said.

"Okay, fine," I said. "I didn't know." I looked down at the dashboard clock. It was nearing eight in the evening. "We've been driving twelve hours," I said. "If I close my eyes, I see the same things I see when they're open."

"*You've* been driving twelve hours. If you'd share the driving, Jeeves, it'd be a lot easier on you."

I let my body go loose as if I were collapsing in despair. We had been through this argument a dozen times in two days. I was terrifically uncomfortable in a car if I wasn't driving. The tension was just unbearable. I constantly watched the road and listened to my heart race. I explained this again and again, but Viv insisted on seeing it as a power issue, a male-female thing, like it was some sort of macho posturing not to let the woman drive. That wasn't it at all. Well, maybe there was a touch of that—my father never even let my mother get a driver's license—but mostly I was just scared when somebody else was driving. Anybody else. I said, "Please don't start, Viv. Just . . . Are we stopping tonight or what?"

Vivian sat up and peered out the window, as if she might be able to see something I couldn't. "I thought we'd be there by now," she said. "I made a reservation at Little America."

"Little America?"

"You'll love it," she said. "Wait and see." Then she said, "Anthony," in a long-drawn-out whine, which I recognized as meaning *Anthony, I have a problem and I need to talk to you about it and I need you to be understanding and loving.*

"What?"

"Anthony," she said. "I'm worried about tonight. I've been worried since this morning."

I had no idea what she was talking about, which wasn't unusual. "Why? What's the problem?"

"Why?" she said. "Do you know how long it's been since we've had sex?"

"A couple of weeks," I said. "I'm keenly aware."

"Three weeks," she said. "Almost a month. I feel like a virgin again. I spent all year building this trip up as a sex holiday; then I get this stupid infection, so you might as well be traveling with a nun; and now, we can finally have sex, and—"

"We can have sex?"

"I'm fine today."

I speeded up a bit.

Vivian said, "Do you see my point?"

"Not really."

"Anthony," she said. "You're so dense. I wanted this to be a romantic trip, and now we've both been waiting and waiting, and I feel like I promised you the Kama Sutra or something. I mean, we can't just have ordinary sex after all this buildup. After all this, I feel like I need to reveal a secret sex organ or some exotic trick you've never dreamed of. I mean, I feel like I need to do the Dance of Seven Veils or something."

"Don't be silly."

"Good," she barked. "Dismiss my anxieties. That'll help a lot."

"Vivian. Honey. First of—"

"Oh, be quiet, Anthony. You're hopeless." She hopped over the seat and into the back of the van, where we had a little traveling room set up. I heard the cot squeak as she climbed on and stretched out. "I'm taking a nap," she said. "Wake me when get to Little America."

"How much longer is that going to be?"

"I thought we'd be there by now. Can't be another five or ten minutes."

"How will I know when we're there?"

"You'll know," she said. "You can't miss it. Believe me."

Three hours later, I made a right turn onto a dirt road that appeared to lead out into the desert. It was after eleven, and I was beginning to feel as though the steering wheel were an extension of my body. Vivian sat alongside me with her knees pulled up to her chin. She was confused. She had fallen asleep a little after eight, and I had pulled into a gas station shortly after that to ask how much longer to Little America. The gas station attendant said, "Little America? About three hundred miles up the road." I said, "Three hundred miles? Are you sure?" He didn't answer. He looked at me as if I had two heads, and then he looked away.

When Vivian finally woke and joined me up front, she wouldn't believe she had so miscalculated the distance to Little America. She snatched the maps from the glove compartment to see for herself. By eleven o'clock we started looking for somewhere to pull off the road so I could sleep a while, and a little after that this dirt road appeared. It didn't look as if it could possibly go anywhere.

Maybe an eighth of a mile off the main road, we found what looked to be an abandoned mine. I parked the van next to a boulder and jumped out as soon as the engine quit. I was dying to stretch, which was the first thing I did as soon as my feet hit the ground. I lifted my hands up high over my head and bent over backward. Joints cracked and popped along my spine and neck. When I straightened up and looked around, I was struck by the stillness of the place. The quiet was amazing. I had never heard such quiet. I must have just stood there motionless for more than a minute, staring out across an endless, rocky plain that looked like the pictures that little robot sent back from the surface of Mars. I was waiting to hear a sound. Anything. I didn't. I didn't hear a damn thing, not even wind. Just . . . nothing, silence. I tried to identify the feeling it evoked and decided it was . . . fear. There was something terrifying about such silence. I thought, This is what it must sound like when you're dead. "Vivian?" I said, as much to hear myself speak as to get her attention.

Vivian was still in the passenger seat. Her arms were crossed over the open window, and she was looking up at the sky. I leaned against the driver's door. "How come it's so quiet?" I asked.

"Isn't it magnificent?" she answered, the awe in her voice palpable.

I looked around, thinking perhaps I had missed something. I

saw the same rocks and heard the same silence. With the exception of the boarded-up mine entrance some twenty feet or so in front of us, this place was the definition of nothing. No sounds. No things. Just dirt, rock, and silence. I said, "If you say so."

She turned around to look at me. "You don't think it's magnificent?" she said. She sounded disappointed in me. "Don't you feel it?"

I decided it would be best not to answer. "Shouldn't there be some sounds?" I asked. "Like, animals scurrying or something? I mean it's just so quiet it's weird. It's not natural."

"There are sounds," she said. "You just can't hear them yet."

I said, "I just can't *hear them* yet?"

She laughed. Apparently she was in a magnanimous mood. "Didn't you say you wanted to sleep awhile?"

"I have to piss first." I looked behind me. The boulder beside the van must have been a good five feet high. I considered walking around to piss on the other side of it. "You sure it's safe out here?" I said. "I mean, there aren't like grizzly bears or tarantulas or anything, right?"

"No grizzly bears in the Wyoming desert," she said. "Might be tarantulas. Long as you don't drag your thing along the ground, you should be fine."

"My *thing*," I said. I walked around to the other side of the boulder and peed, being careful to keep my *thing* a good distance back from the rock, lest something should leap up on it. I was definitely jumpy. It was the silence and expanse of the sky. It seemed to press down on me. Even the stars seemed too bright and too numerous.

"Hey, Vivian," I called, my eyes fixed on the powdery surface of the rock. "Maybe we should forget the nap and just keep going till we get to this Little America place."

On the other side of the boulder, the back doors of the van popped open. "You need to sleep a bit," Vivian said, from the back of the van. "Unless you want to let me drive, of course."

I made a face, as if she could see me.

"That's what I thought," she said.

I was getting bored watching a little river form near my feet. "What's with this Little America?" I said. "What kind of name is that for a motel?"

"It's not a motel," her voice came back. "It's more a resort: green grass and neat little clean buildings . . . you know, like idealized, hometown America, only it's stuck in the middle of the desert."

"Green?" I said. "Grass?" I was suddenly enthusiastic. I realized that I hadn't seen anything green in days.

"I knew you'd love it," she said. "Just don't ask how much water they have to waste to grow lawns in the desert."

I hadn't planned on asking. It didn't seem like a waste to me. I zipped up and walked around the boulder thinking about grass and trees and how much I took them for granted. When I reached the back of the van, however, my thoughts shifted quickly. Vivian was stretched out naked on the cot. In the desert moonlight, the hidden flesh of her body, ordinarily pale white, even pinkish, appeared dark and exotic. Her nipples, reddish under the light of lamps and ceiling fixtures, were darker, a deep maroon or brown. She was smiling just slightly, and her eyes were full of playful invitation. I sat on the bumper and had my clothes off in seconds, and a few minutes later, we were making love. The little cot creaked and the van shook. Then, at the sweetest, deepest moment of penetration, I felt something bite me where it should have been impossible to get bitten. I stopped moving abruptly. A bad joke about vaginas and teeth came to mind. In a husky voice,

Vivian asked me if anything was wrong. I kissed her on the cheek. I pushed again and there it was again, a distinct, a definite bite, in response to which I jerked back quickly. I came out of her and looked down, and it took me a good several seconds of staring to realize what I was looking at. "Vivian," I said. "I found that blue cap that was missing."

Vivian jumped up into a sitting position and looked for herself. "What have you done?" she said. "What the hell is that?"

The previously missing blue cap was suctioned tight to the tip of my penis, looking like a doll-sized, cutesy Shriner's hat worn jauntily, a little off to one side. "I didn't do anything," I said. "It must have been . . . in there . . . and when I . . ."

"Oh . . ." She appeared to be at a loss for words. I had a hard time reading her expression. I couldn't tell whether she thought this was funny or tragic. "God," she said, looking down at herself as if she were looking at someplace foreign. "What else is in there?"

I said, "It must have been from when you—"

"I know what happened," she said. "I just can't believe . . . I mean, I didn't feel anything. I didn't think there was that much . . . *room* in there."

"Me neither," I said. "It must be . . . capacious."

Vivian looked at me a moment as if I might be dangerous. I gathered she didn't think I was very funny.

"Viv . . ." I touched her shoulder.

She kept staring at me. Her face seemed to be collapsing. Her eyes grew teary. "Anthony," she said. "I don't know about us getting married." She slid down off the cot and out of the van. She walked casually to the boulder, as if she were fully dressed and strolling down a corridor to the ladies' room, and not naked and walking to a rock in the desert.

I followed her—after gingerly removing the little man's cap. It was odd. We were padding around the desert as if it were our bedroom.

"Can I have a moment of privacy," she said when I tried to talk to her.

"Sure," I said, and I waited on my side of the boulder. It struck me that this was a lot like the arguments we'd have in my apartment, when she'd go into the bathroom and I'd have to talk to her through the closed door.

I touched a slick space on the boulder with a fingertip. The surface was smooth as skin. "Vivian," I said. "What have I done?"

"What have you done?" she repeated. "Do you know how this makes me feel?"

"The cap thing? It's nothing. It's funny."

"*The cap thing . . . It's funny . . .* Anthony," she said, "you're insensitive."

"Oh, Vivian . . . Look. I'm sorry. I didn't mean to be insensitive. Truly."

"First it's the infection," she said. "Then my vagina turns out to be a storage closet—"

I laughed.

"You think it's funny?"

I stopped laughing. "That wasn't supposed to be funny?"

She didn't answer, but I could feel the waves of anger right through the boulder. "Okay," I said. "I'm a jerk. I'm sorry."

"You're an insensitive jerk."

"Okay. An insensitive jerk."

"It's not just this," she said. "The cap thing. It's the past two days. It's the West."

"The West?"

"Ever since we've gotten to the real West, the real empty spaces, you've done nothing but complain."

I turned around and leaned back against the boulder. I looked up at the endless expanse of sky. "That's not true," I said.

"Yes it is. Not only have you not been impressed, you act like you're offended by the landscape, like you can't believe God had the gall to create such a place."

"You're exaggerating."

"I am not. You've been whining for two days."

"What do you want from me, Vivian? I'm uncomfortable here. This is not my home."

"No," she said. "Your home's in Manhattan, where you're the Golden Boy, the hotshot TV writer, the man with the fawning friends."

"Don't start."

"Well, this is *my* home." she said. "This is where *I* feel like somebody."

"Fine," I said. "It's your home. It's still ugly."

"It's not ugly, Anthony," she responded, calmly. "You just lack the spirit necessary to comprehend the beauty of the West."

"I 'lack the spirit' . . . How long have you been composing that?" I was looking directly at the boulder at that point, talking to the surface of the rock. Then, just as the thought occurred to me that maybe she was right, maybe we should rethink the wedding, she came around from her side of the rock like opening a door. "I haven't been composing it," she said. "It just came to me. I just suddenly realized it, why you were having so much trouble with the West."

"Oh," I said. "So now you've got me figured out."

She gave me one of her coy smiles. She looked me over. "See

what the West does?" she said. "Even a guy like you winds up walking around naked under the stars."

"A guy like me?"

Vivian said, "Don't get petulant," and then went back into the van.

When I didn't follow immediately, she said, "Come on, Anthony. Let's finish what we started."

She knew that would get me. I went back to the van, and we took up where we had left off. When we were done, and I was lying on my back, exhausted, with sleep hovering only moments away, I opened my eyes and saw she was looking down at me, observing me. She ran her fingers through my hair and placed the palm of her hand on my cheek. I was too tired to respond, which is the way I get after good sex, just useless, absent of all energy. I closed my eyes. I remember thinking, *I don't understand this woman.* I found that unsettling, given that we were getting married, but then my thoughts shifted again, and I was picturing Little America as a place of green lawns and comfortable beds and two-story houses with bay windows where aproned women watched birds eat seed out of wooden feeders. The predominant color was green. *That* I found comforting—and I laughed at myself, at how absurdly old-fashioned some deep part of me was. When I tried to imagine one of those aproned women searching around inside herself for a lost medicine cap, I laughed again.

Vivian said, gently, "What are you laughing at?"

I managed to mutter "Nothing," and I touched her hand, which was still resting on my cheek, to assure her everything was fine.

She said, "I'm driving tomorrow, Anthony." She sounded the way she did often after sex, all soft and gentle and loving. Her voice seemed to drift down to me from the upper edge of a circle that was just the two of us walled off from all that vast emptiness outside.

"Okay," I said. "Sure. You drive tomorrow."

Vivian didn't say anything. She pulled the back doors closed and cuddled up beside me, and then I let myself float deliciously toward sleep thinking about Little America somewhere off in the distance. In my mind, the words hummed round and round like a meaningless song, a tune full of vacant yearning out in the desert: "Little America," they said. "Little America, Little America, Little America . . ."

Smothered Mate

STEPHANIE PLAYED A KING'S PAWN OPENING, AS USUAL, AND Jay played the Sicilian in response, as usual, and then the game proceeded along predictably careful lines until Jay moved his knight aggressively to g4, in front of Steph's castled king. Stephanie considered the position for a moment before turning away from the board, shifting around in her seat and looking at the ceiling as if trying to see out to the roof. They were in the spacious kitchen of her apartment, above an art gallery on North Moore, in Tribeca. "I just realized," she said, "I didn't pack Lucian's iPhone."

"Is that your responsibility?" Jay asked. "Packing the iPhone?" Then he added, "What the hell's an iPhone?"

Stephanie said, "What planet do you live on?" She sounded more distracted than interested. Without waiting for an answer, she got up and went to the bedroom. "I can still catch him at the office," she said, mostly to herself.

Jay reviewed the position. Through a tall kitchen window next to the table, the dull light of an overcast day spread over a handsome, rosewood chessboard, with inlaid squares and crisp black and white Staunton pieces, hand carved and triple weighted. Steph needed only to threaten his knight by moving her pawn to h3 and he'd have to pull it back. He got up from the table, went to the fridge, and poured himself a glass of orange juice. From the bedroom, down a long, high-ceilinged corridor, where Steph was talking to Lucian on the phone, her voice sounded like someone speaking from underground. She was apologizing, asking Lucian to forgive her, and Jay could tell from her tone, her curt, choked pleading, that Lucian was lighting into her for forgetting to pack the phone. From the black surface of the fridge, encased in a magnetically attached plastic frame, Stephanie smiled up at him, looking both more youthful than her thirty-two years, in the unmarred skin of her face, in the lustrous fall of wispy blonde hair, and much, much older, in the world-weary cast of her smile, the longing in her eyes. Beside her, his arm around her, Lucian grinned mischievously.

Lucian was one of those people whose appearance uncannily matches their personality. He was a surly, habitually miserable cynic, blind entirely to any hint of goodness in the world, paranoid, mean, and impossible to like—and that's how he looked. He was average height, five-ten, five-eleven, but he was perpetually hunched over, as if weighted down by the burden of his disposition. His hair was always unkempt, his clothes rumpled, and his face scrunched up as if something were hurting him. In his mid-forties, he was a parody of a curmudgeon. When a computer dating program paired him with Stephanie, and he first met her for dinner, and she didn't immediately run away, he had assumed she was only interested in his money and position—and he told her so. Later, when he found out about the bombing, when she told him about her body, he asked her to spend the night. It was as if, having learned her secret, he for the first time considered the possibility that someone as attractive as Stephanie might genuinely be interested in him. After Steph spent the night, and that went as well as could be hoped for, he proposed marriage and she accepted. They had been together at this point—on this Sunday afternoon of the weekly chess game—for a little more than five years.

Stephanie and Jay had met three years before the marriage, on a Sunday afternoon in Brooklyn. The first time they saw each other, they were both on fire. The flames seemed to be—weirdly, eerily—consuming only specific portions of their bodies. Stephanie was on fire from her feet to her shoulders, yet her neck and arms and face were untouched. The fire clung to her and seemed to be burning hot but without flames. Jay's crotch and thighs and feet were burning, and no other part of him. They were both screaming and running pointlessly through smoke and darkness that had been, an instant earlier, a Brooklyn coffeehouse, where they had come to hear a young bluesy singer-musician who had died instantly in the explosion, the firebomb intended primarily for him and situated directly under the stage where he was performing, placed there by a fan who believed his lyrics were commands from the devil ordering her to do exactly what she did: learn how to construct an incendiary device with white phosphorous and use it to burn up the musician and his followers. Most of what happened that afternoon was only figured out much later. That Stephanie and Jay were the two burning figures who ran into each other and, literally, embraced, probably in some partly instinctive, partly hysterical, partly accidental attempt to extinguish the flames, only came out months later, in what was essentially a group therapy session with the eighteen survivors of a firebombing that killed thirty-three people, not a single one of them yet out of their twenties.

Burning Man

For both Steph and Jay, it was the last thing they remembered of the bombing, and they concluded it must have happened within seconds after the explosion. Neither of them talked about it much anymore, but over the years they had worked out the details. The small, cavernous space of the coffeehouse, dimly lit, a dozen tables and a few rows of chairs. A chord, a few notes picked to begin a song, and then a kind of instantaneous transformation of space during which the stage became a bright light. The order of the room—the carefully arranged tables, the lined-up chairs— did a kaleidoscopic dance of rearrangement, and Stephanie and Jay rose up on fire and embraced.

Stephanie came back from the bedroom, glanced at Jay leaning against the kitchen counter next to the fridge, and then gripped a corner of the table in her hands and leaned over the chessboard as if she were about to dive into its engaging geometry of squares and pieces. She wore khaki slacks and a long-sleeved cotton shirt, green with a button-down collar. She was five-nine, exactly the same height as Jay. Every part of her that wasn't hidden under her clothes was youthful and pretty: her face, which was slightly long and made her look serious, as if she should be a professor or a classical musician; her hair, blonde and shoulder length, obsessively pampered by creams and conditioners and salon appointments; her hands and her long thin fingers, jewelry-less except for a plain gold wedding band. She stood in the light from the window, the whole of her, body and mind, absorbed in the arrangement of black and white chess pieces on a board of sixty-four squares. Most of what she kept covered he had never seen, except for her arms, and from that, and from his own body, he could imagine the rest of the disfigurement. She had undergone twelve operations in the years after the bombing. He'd had five. The surgeons had removed what had been left of his genitals, and what was there now even he couldn't bear to see. His burned skin was like the skin of her arms, a doughy swamp of swellings and scars. Like Stephanie, he was blessed in that his face wasn't badly damaged. After some minor surgery he looked pretty much the way he'd always looked.

Stephanie said, her eyes still fixed on the board, "He can be such an asshole sometimes."

Jay said, "Sometimes?"

Stephanie whispered "stop," and then threatened his knight, as he expected, but with pawn to f3, which opened up the possibility of a diagonal check with the queen, which in turn made possible a combination of moves that could lead to a checkmate.

"F3?" he said, across the room, still leaning on the fridge.

"Problem?" Steph looked down at the board again, as if trying to figure out what she did wrong.

Jay returned to his seat at the table and Steph settled in across from him. They were both quiet then, staring at the chess pieces and the board as if there were an absorbing movie playing on a screen only they could see. Outside, a truck rumbled by, making the window glass rattle.

Jay knew his next move would be to check with the queen, but he was taking his time playing through Steph's possible responses. She was the better chess player, and he hadn't won a game in months, but he thought he had her now. As far as he could determine, the only way to prevent the mate required exchanging her rook for his knight, which would leave him with a significant advantage. He took his time looking over the position, wanting to be sure he wasn't missing something.

"So?" Steph said. "You put me in check." She made a quick, small gesture with her hands that said "So what?"

Jay moved the queen to b6. "Check," he said, and then added, "Why do you put up with him, Steph? Seriously. Why don't you tell him to come home and get his own fucking iPhone-whatever and stick it up his ass?"

Stephanie smiled first and then laughed. She was still looking at the board. "I should," she said. "He'd go ballistic."

"So? Why don't you?"

"And then what would we do?" She looked up, pulling herself momentarily out of the game. "If my marriage broke up," she said, "what would we do?"

Jay returned his attention to the board. For the past six months, since he had quit the last in a long series of bullshit jobs, Stephanie had been paying his rent, embezzling the money out of credit cards and household accounts. It wasn't difficult. Lucian made more money than the three of them could spend in multiple lifetimes.

Stephanie said again, "What would we do, Jay?"

Jay felt his eyes beginning to get wet, and he hated himself for it. To make the tears go away, he tapped into his anger, which was always there. "You'd have plenty of money after a divorce," he said. "You'd come out of it rich, and you know it."

"I'm not talking about money," she said, and her voice went up a little and got louder, as if she were insulted that he'd even suggest money was the issue.

Jay gestured to the board and fixed his eyes on the position. He said, "It's your move, Steph. Just go, okay?"

"Jay," Stephanie said, and in the pleading way she said his name there was a single question. All he had to do was look up at her to answer it. "Jay," she said again, insisting. When she reached over the chessboard to touch him, he pulled away from her. He slid back in his chair and closed his eyes as if that might make him disappear. "No," she said. "Of course not." Then there were several moments of silence in which Jay knew she was watching him, looking across the table at a thirty-five-year-old man, a man who looked normal as the next guy in his sneakers and jeans and dark knit shirt. She watched him where he sat rigid in his seat with his eyes closed, unable to open them, unable to look back at her. Finally, she said, "Forget it, Jay," and her voice softened to gentle. "Jay," she said, "I'm moving. Look."

At the sound of a piece moving on the chessboard, Jay opened his eyes and fell back into the game. She had moved her king to h1, out of check. He moved his knight to f2, putting her in check again, and then she had to take with the rook, exchanging it for the knight—but she didn't. She moved her king to g1, and from there it was a forced mate in three, which he announced, softly.

"Where?" she said. "I don't see it."

Jay showed her the three forced moves, including a sacrifice of the queen, that led to a smothered mate, a mate delivered by the knight, the king surrounded by his own pieces simply having nowhere to go.

"That's gorgeous," Stephanie said. She smiled, appreciative of the combination's elegance and finality. "I didn't see it coming," she added, and then, as if she was suddenly tired and needed a moment to rest, she folded her hands in front of her on the table and bowed her head. Across from her, Jay did the same. Together, they looked like a family at prayer, two people lost in a quiet moment of reverence. Outside, several car horns screamed angrily at each other. The shrill noise beat against the kitchen window.

Burning Man

Burning Man was heat, dust, and madness, and I felt about as out of place as it's possible to feel, in my middle-aged body, in my khaki shorts and knit shirt and sandals, in my expanding belly and soft chest and salt-and-pepper hair cut short, surrounded by the extraordinarily young and youthful with extravagant manes of vibrant hair and muscular, ripe bodies, either mostly undressed or wildly costumed in getups that ranged from Fellini to Mad Max. I'd been at the Labor Day weekend Festival of the Burning Man for two days. I was about to meet my brother, whom I hadn't seen in more than ten years. I was with a young woman named Chrysalis, no last name, whom I'd met as soon as I arrived at the festival. I pulled up in my Volkswagen camper, parked, and got out to look around at the Black Rock Desert, which is an amazingly flat expanse of cracked mud, and she was standing there, a waif of a girl in fat metallic boots over silvery quilted space-suit pants that came up to her hips and left her hard stomach bare between their Velcro-tab top and the bottom of a bright yellow halter. A massive, framed backpack hovered over her shoulders like a small building. She struggled under the weight of it. I asked if I could be of any assistance, and she shook her head and said no, but that she was just about to set up camp. I told her I hadn't seen her when I pulled up, and I offered to find another spot, but she looked me over and then smiled and said No, it'd be okay, and we went about setting up our encampments and thus became neighbors.

My brother had given me instructions to meet him near the burning man, a forty-foot-high wooden statue that was soon to burn while ten to fifteen thousand onlookers danced and screamed and did God-knows-what, certainly lots of drugs. I was looking forward to it. If it weren't for Johnny, my brother, I'd have never known of the existence of the festival. It was much more his kind of thing than mine. My brother was a public figure, a rock-and-roll bad boy known all over the world as Splay—guitar player, singer, public madman, and pervert from the band of the same name. I was a writer of stories and novels; and since I had made a comfortable career for myself in academia, it behooved me to keep my relationship to Splay quiet. Splay was famous enough that if people had known he was my brother, it would have changed my life. Whatever accomplishments I managed on my own would be colored by my relationship to Splay. I'd be Kevin Perry, the writer who was Splay's younger brother. I'd walk out the door of my suburban ranch house outside Iowa City, and I'd find reporters and photographers looking to get my reaction every time Splay got in trouble, which, thankfully, was happening with less frequency as he got older. Splay was forty-seven. He was still famous—but not as. I hadn't told Chrysalis about him. She knew I was meeting my brother, his name was Johnny, and he'd be wearing a big red sombrero. And that was all she knew.

"More than ten years," she said. "How come you haven't seen him in so long?"

"Falling out," I said. "Family thing."

"What about?" She tucked her hands into her pants, just slid them down under the waistband, so that the heels of her hands were resting on her bare hip bones. She was wearing big boots and fat pants again, astronaut pants. Same outfit as when we first met, only the halter top was blue—soft, watery, cerulean blue.

"It's a long, long story," I said, and I touched her elbow, signaling her to stop a moment. We were nearing the center of the series of concentric circles that formed the structural pattern of Burning Man. There were a couple of roads—aisles kept clear of encampments—that pierced the circles of vans and campers and tents and lean-tos and what-nots where masses of people were living for the weekend. Often the housing—which ranged from pup tents and trailers to wildly imagined temporary structures made of old parachutes and sticks and scrap metal—was itself arranged in circles, providing a wagon-train effect. We had just passed an encampment where several young women were showering under a line of plastic camp-shower bags hanging from a free-standing construction of tubes and pipes, and it had taken all my willpower not to stop and gawk at their tanned bodies, and especially at the places where the tan disappeared, where they looked as though they were wearing white-skin bikinis. But I didn't stare. I walked on by as if I often strolled past women showering in the sun.

Chrysalis said, "Do you see him?"

"Chrys," I said. "Tell me the truth. How ridiculously out of place do I really look?"

"Oh, chill." She hooked her arm through mine and pulled me along. "You're a writer. You're the real thing. You don't have to get dressed up."

I had given Chrysalis a copy of my most recent novel within an hour of having met her. I explained that I was recently divorced from my second wife, and that I was in the process of rethinking my life. She told me that she was an artist and an elementary school teacher. She was also divorced, though her marriage had only lasted a few months. It had ended as soon as she told her artist-husband, whom she had been with since they were both sophomores in college, that she was pregnant. He took off. She had an abortion. That was a little over a year ago. She was twenty-two. "It's not as bad as it sounds," she had said. "I didn't want a kid either. I wasn't ready."

As we continued walking toward the towering wooden man, I relaxed a bit, pleased she had hooked her arm through mine, which was our first physical contact. We strolled in silence, arm in arm. Then she said, "You never answered my question," and leaned into me playfully, nudging my shoulder with her cheek. "What was the falling out about? With your brother?"

I didn't know what to tell her. I didn't like the idea of lying, but I wasn't ready yet to tell her my brother was Splay—and I couldn't figure out how to explain why I hadn't seen Johnny in so long without revealing his stage identity. I hadn't seen him since the eighties. Once he figured out—which didn't take him long, he's bright enough—that I was embarrassed by him, he stayed out of my life. I feel bad about this, but not that bad. You can't do the things Splay does—or did, at least—and not expect some consequences. He's masturbated on stage, for one. Offstage, he was arrested twice for statutory rape. Ten years ago he became world-famous for having oral sex, onstage, with one of rock's multimillionaires, some guy named Fey Wrey, after the old screen actress, the one from *King Kong*. It was after that performance we stopped talking to each other altogether. This other guy, Fey, he turned his back to the audience in the middle of an unending guitar riff and made the obvious motion of opening his fly—this is all on camera—and then Splay walked onstage and knelt at his feet and gave him a blow job, or at least they made it look that way. Before the show was over they were both arrested, yanked off the stage, and for the next couple of years they were household names. Your local priest, your Episcopalian minister: they knew all about Splay and Fey. Everyone did. His CD sales broke records. He made many millions. So he was famous and rich, and one of the minor prices he paid was that he no longer talked to his brother, who was embarrassed by him. Our parents were already both gone at that point, which was in some ways a blessing.

I was still pondering how to answer Chrys when I spotted a pair of red sombreros bobbing in our direction. "I'll have to tell you another time," I said.

Chrys had already seen the sombreros. "I thought you just said your brother?"

"I'm not surprised," I said. "He's usually got somebody with him."

When we were about to walk right past each other, I stopped and smiled at Johnny, and he recognized me. He returned the smile and caught the woman with him by the wrist and turned her toward us. I offered Johnny my hand and we shook and then stepped back from each other. I put my hands on my hips and Johnny crossed his arms under his chest, and we just stood there looking at each other until the woman with him gestured toward a makeshift, mock refreshment stand and said, "McSatans anyone?"

I said, "Sure," and we all four started for McSatans, a corrugated tin and scrap wood McDonalds parody, complete with cardboard cutout golden arches, where a couple of guys were giving away juice and sandwiches. McSatans was located a bit back from the stream of people, and on the way we completed the introductions. Johnny introduced the woman with him as Melinda—Mel for short. I introduced Chrysalis as a friend, not bothering to explain we had only just met at the festival.

Johnny was dressed handsomely in a white linen suit over a wine red shirt. His hair was cut short, much like mine, only it was a lustrous blond, far from my 50-50 mix of dark brown and gray. I was tempted to say, "Hey, I used to know you when you had brown hair," but I didn't. For all his expensive clothes and hair care, Johnny still didn't look too good, at least not to me. He was thin, and his features were pinched, as if he were tense about something. He seemed jumpy and edgy and simultaneously tired—as if he really wanted to catch some sleep but was afraid of something. I figured it was some drug he was on. He was still a world-class stoner. According to the tabloids, he was a heroin addict.

"Johnny," I said. "You look like Tom Wolfe."

"Tom who?"

"*Electric Kool-Aid Acid Test.*"

Mel said, to Johnny, "It's a book. Tom Wolfe wrote it." Then to me: "Your brother doesn't get much time to read."

"Chrysalis," Johnny said, disregarding me. His eyes moved up and down Chrys with no subtlety at all, as if he were examining a potential purchase.

I said, "Chrysalis is an artist."

Mel smiled, and Johnny made a grunting noise.

I looked hard at Johnny, trying to read him. There was something decidedly different about him. He seemed . . . less intelligent. He had, almost, the look of the dim-witted, someone who had to think a second or two to form a word. But the Johnny

I knew was anything but dim-witted. Of the two of us, he was smarter: things came to him more easily. He did better in school. He was quicker. On the street, out with the kids, he was my protector. If I had a problem, Johnny'd always know how to handle it. We used to walk home from school together most days, side by side on neat suburban walkways bracketed by lawns. A couple of school kids, quiet usually, caught up in dreams. We were always big dreamers. We had that in common.

"Johnny," I said. "You're looking tired."

"You're the one should be tired." He leered at Chrys a moment and then grinned at me.

"Don't mind him," Mel said. "All he can ever think about is sex." She seemed amused. "You know his reputation," she said, giving Chrys a between-women look.

"Actually," I said. "She doesn't."

Mel said, "Oh," and Johnny grunted, and they both looked as though I had just answered a question for them.

Chrys said, "Something I should know?"

Mel said, "Why don't you come back to our trailer with us? We can get something decent to eat." She was wearing a bright white sundress, with red flowers to match the sombrero. She was a woman in her forties, at least. There were lines around her eyes and mouth that showed her age, but she was still attractive—and she had obviously once been stunning.

"Shit," Johnny said, and he looked at me. "This heat's fucking with me, Kev. I need a siesta."

Mel put her arm around Johnny's waist.

Johnny said to Mel, "It's the fucking heat."

"It is hot," Mel said, and she seemed suddenly anxious to get Johnny away. "Why don't you two come by a little later? We'll send someone for you."

Johnny turned to Chrys. "Chrysalis," he said, his grin overtly lascivious. "See you later."

And then they walked away into a moving line of people and disappeared.

When they were out of sight, I said, "That was weird, wasn't it?"

"About as weird as you get." Chrys seemed to think about it a moment, and then she laughed. "They'll send someone for us? Is your brother, like, an escapee from an asylum?"

Chrys seemed amused, but on the verge of deciding we were all lunatics: Johnny and Mel, and me along with them. "It's a long story," I said. "Maybe I should explain a few things to you."

"Good idea."

We started back to our encampment.

Chrys said, "I can't believe the way he was coming on to me—with his girlfriend right there. Not to mention you. I mean, he must figure we're together. No?"

"He was outrageous," I said. "Are you offended?"

"Guys," she said. "You're all crazy. You should meet Mr. Miller, our assistant principal."

Then it was my turn to laugh. I said, "I find it hard to think of you as a school teacher."

"What you are?" she said. "*You're* a school teacher."

"I didn't say it was hard to think of me as a teacher. That's not hard at all."

"So why is it hard to think of me?"

I didn't respond right away. I was considering not responding at all, seeing if she might be willing to let the subject drop. It was obvious I had hit a sore spot. Suddenly her shoulders were stiff and her face was tight, her lips pressed together. Suddenly, from under her sexy blue halter and space-suit pants, from under her hard body and youthful skin, I saw the schoolmarm emerging, the woman she had the potential to become: stiff and cold and bitter. It was distressing. I turned my best smile on her. "Because you're so young and beautiful," I said, trying to sound comically flirtatious, "because you seem way too stunningly gorgeous, like you should be a movie star or—"

She shoved me. "Stop it," she said. "Tell me the truth." The stiffness disappeared and she returned to her youthful self, though she still seemed worried. She stepped closer to me and hooked her arm through mine. We were walking with the crowd, in a stream of people, and when a young man walking toward us caught Chrys's eye and smiled at her, she ignored him. "You think it's a mistake, my teaching, being this young and teaching? I mean, if I want to be an artist, shouldn't I be in Paris or something, being decadent, hanging out with Van Gogh types—instead of Mr. Miller, who's always copping feels off me whenever the hallway's crowded?"

I said, "Look around, Chrys. Look where you are!" At that moment we were walking past an elaborate castlelike structure, complete with moat and drawbridge, and a pair of young women dressed in shimmering veils dancing on the battlements. "Van Gogh would have cut off his other ear for a chance to hang out here for a weekend."

Chrys brightened at that notion. She smiled genuinely. "This is wild, this place, isn't it?"

We had been moving away from the center of Burning Man, back toward our encampment, but there was still craziness going on all around us—and a tangible sense of growing excitement as the day wore on toward the climactic burning, which would happen some time after dark. All around us there was dancing, and little parades, and singing and music. It felt to me like a

Bourbon Street of the Alternative Culture, Bourbon Street picked up and dropped in the middle of the desert. "Wild, absolutely," I answered. "But too hot. Must be a hundred and ten. I'm looking forward to my air-conditioning." We were nearing the van and the tent. "Why don't you come in and take a nap with me," I said. "It'll be too hot in your tent."

"A nap?"

"Sure," I said. "A siesta!"

Chrys seemed amused with me. "A siesta," she repeated. "Right." She pointed at the van, which was now directly alongside us. "Honk when it's cool," she said. "It'll be a blast oven in there." She went on to her tent and threw back the flap, and then crawled in.

I had left all the van's windows open a crack, so it wasn't exactly a blast oven—but it was close. I cranked it up and turned on the air, and in short order it was cool enough to climb in and straighten things out a bit. I liked my van. It was one of the few possessions I took away from the divorce. Kay, my ex-wife—my *second* ex-wife—was an entirely domestic creature: a woman of minivans and suburban houses, of Little League and den motherdom. She had grown up with generous, well-to-do parents and gone to an Ivy League school, and married and had two children, and then divorced and then remarried and then divorced again. Currently, she was not in good shape. Men kept disappointing Kay. Soon after she married for the first time, her father divorced her mother and married a younger woman, a business associate; approximately five years later, Kay's husband divorced her, when he met a younger woman who didn't mind that he was an alcoholic; and then, ten years later, she divorced me, when a student I had slept with showed up at our front door, wanting to have a talk with her. The fact that I was deeply sorry about what had happened, that I hadn't intended for it to happen, that it had been a onetime thing, a mistake I swore would never happen again—all that made no difference. Kay had had it with men. When that girl showed up at the door, I was gone. Kay pitched my stuff out the windows, literally. I drove away in the camper.

All that happened about a year ago. Drew, the student I had slept with, thought she was in love with me. I knew she was an emotional basket-case, but when I found myself alone with her one night on a street corner in Iowa City, and she invited me back to her apartment . . . I went. The next evening, at dinnertime, with our kids at the dinner table, Drew came knocking at the door. She felt it was best to get everything out in the open right away. She felt Kay needed to know I loved her, Drew, and I was going to leave her, Kay—which is what, God help me, I had told Drew the night before. And that was that. I'm lucky Kay still lets me see the kids.

This situation would have been bad for anyone, but, in my case, I had left my first wife several years earlier for an almost perfect reversal of my betrayal. My first wife was Kay's opposite. She was raised poor and wild and was hanging out with artists and musicians by the time she was sixteen. She was twenty-five when I married her and already world-weary. I left her when I found out she was having an affair with one of her students. I despised her for it.

I knew what betrayal felt like. I didn't want to do it. I didn't think I would. And then I hated myself when I did.

It was not a good time. I got in touch with Johnny after I was living alone for a few months, on a night when I was feeling particularly bad for myself, being so isolated and so estranged from everyone I had ever loved, including my only brother. I told him

Burning Man

what a mess I was, how unhappy I was, that I needed to see him again. The first space Johnny could open in his calendar was Labor Day weekend, Festival of the Burning Man.

And now . . . here I was. I tidied up the back of the van, unzipping and spreading out my pillows and sleeping bags over sheet-covered foam cushions. Then I honked the horn, and pulled out a few books, and made myself comfortable. I stretched out and looked through tinted windows at a bright blue sky. A minute later, Chrys tapped at the back door, then pulled it open and climbed in.

"Ummm," she said. "This is a lot better. My tent is broiling." She sat up, with her back against the front seat, and pulled off her boots. "You were going to explain a few things," she said. "Remember?"

"Oh, right," I said. "About Johnny."

"Right. About Johnny." She pulled off her pants, revealing slight, bikini panties, and then the halter top, revealing her breasts, before climbing under the sleeping bag–blanket and pulling it up to her chin. She undressed as perfunctorily as if I had been her longtime roommate.

It took me a second to steady my breathing. I wanted nothing more than to feel the weight of her breasts in my hands. "Give me a second," I said. "I need to recover."

She smiled playfully. "Come on under here with me."

"Come on under there with you," I repeated, exaggerating the stunned disbelief I legitimately felt. "Sounds good to me." I undid my belt buckle and started getting out of my clothes while she watched.

"Your brother," she said, reminding me to explain.

"My brother . . . ," I hesitated a moment, folding my shorts and tossing them toward the back of the van. "My brother is rich," I said. "And as we all know, the rich are not like the rest of us."

"How rich?"

"Megarich. Hundreds-of-millions rich."

"Hundreds? Really? From what? What's he do?"

"Music industry."

"What's he do in the music industry?"

"Long story," I said, and pulled the sleeping bag up and slid under. I was naked from the waist down. I hadn't taken off my shirt because I didn't want to expose all that soft, unmuscular flesh.

Chrys cuddled against me as soon as I was under the blankets, and then the conversation ended. She took a condom out of a leather change purse and handed it to me, and we were making love within minutes. I finished way too soon, leaving her not even close to being satisfied. I was embarrassed, but she seemed okay about it. I tried to finish by touching her, but she wouldn't let me. "No," she said. "That's so mechanical."

"I feel like a kid," I said. "Like an inexperienced boy."

She kissed me gently, lovingly, on the forehead. "An inexperienced boy," she said, "wouldn't have a clue there was a problem."

"You have a point there." I settled myself down into my pillow. I wanted to tell her I loved her. I felt the words knocking at some inner door, asking to be let out. I didn't speak them. But I felt them. I closed my eyes.

I didn't fall asleep, but I could tell by the way Chrys appeared when I peeked that she thought I had. She looked around the van, taking things in, observing. She pulled a copy of my last book out from between the front seats and read the back cover. I let her think I was sleeping because I was afraid she might want to make love again—and I knew there was no way. I wasn't sure how much

Chrys knew about older men. When she got dressed quietly and sneaked out of the van, careful not to wake me, I was relieved. I turned onto my back and lay with my arms crossed under my head. I contemplated the possibility of a serious relationship with Chrys, and the difference in our ages quickly came up as a major problem. But then, I knew middle-aged men marry younger women all the time.

For a moment, I let myself imagine what it might be like if I were to live with, or even marry, Chrys—and all the complaints about me from the women I had lived with came to mind immediately. I was moody and sullen and wrapped up in my writing. I was temperamental and persnickety. And it was true. When I wasn't writing, I was miserable. I'd wake up some mornings absolutely furious, as if on fire with a rage I couldn't name or identify. I'd be irritable and combative. And when I was writing, I was anxious, anxious that I wouldn't get the story right, that I wouldn't tell it the way it had to be told—or that something would get in the way of my writing, that I'd have to drive someone to the airport, or one of the kids would have to stay home from school with a fever and I'd have to look after him. I'd worry I was really a miserable writer, that I couldn't find the truth in a story if it were flaming in front of my eyes. But, still, she seemed to appreciate that I was a writer. It was possible she'd be willing to put up with me—or, even, that I might be capable of changing.

I didn't get a lot of time to follow this train of thought before Mel approached the back of the van, peered in through the tinted glass, and knocked. She was wearing the same white sundress with red flowers, but she had lost the red sombrero, and I noticed how attractively her auburn hair was cut and styled. She wore it short and parted left of center. As she turned her head, it moved uniformly, in waves, with the fluidity of water. I opened the back door and she climbed in, smiling brightly. She said, "Hello, Kevin," and looked down at the second pillow and the mussed blankets beside me. "Where's Chrys?"

"In her tent." I pointed out the window. "Where's Johnny?"

She sat with her legs tucked under her and her hands folded in her lap. "You know you're the only one other than me who calls him Johnny?"

"*Splay*..." I tried out the sound of the word. "I can't imagine it."

Mel looked at me as if she found me slightly mystifying.

"Who are you exactly to Johnny? If you don't mind my asking?"

"*Exactly?* That's hard to say with a guy like Johnny. I'm his companion."

"How long," I asked, "have you been his companion?"

"About ten years," she answered, punctuating her words by cocking her head and smiling with an exaggerated brightness, which was amusing, as she obviously intended.

"Jesus," I said. "You could be his wife."

"Well," she said. "I suppose I am, common law. Sure. I'm his wife." She had a look on her face that was a mixture of mirth and surprise. She seemed to find me funny—and a little odd. She added, "I'm also his pimp, his drug supplier, housekeeper, financier, secretary, gofer. . . . You name it."

"Pimp?"

"Sure." She took a deep breath, signaling that she was about to launch into a long explanation. "Everybody," she said, "wants to fuck Johnny—but they all think he's got AIDS—which he doesn't, by the way. I make sure they know that, that he doesn't have AIDS. I bring it up in conversation . . . '*Man,*' I'll say, '*I make Splay get an AIDS test every six months, long as he wants to fuck me.*' Then I'll show them the results of the last test. . . . And it's all true. I do make him get an AIDS test every six months if he wants to fuck me, which he does every once in a while."

"*Everybody?*" I said. "Wants to fuck Johnny?"

"Oh, God . . . You don't want to hear," she said, with an air of confidentiality, as if there were things she'd love to tell me. "Absolutely. Everybody. You shocked? He's *your* brother."

"That he is," I said, and I had no idea what to say next. I sat there with my legs stretched out in front of me, barefoot, wearing shorts and a T-shirt, looking, I imagined, as unhip as I felt.

"So," Mel said. "Why don't you get Chrys, and we can . . . ?" She gestured off into the distance, in the direction from which she had come.

I said, "Why don't you get her?" and I opened the back door for her. "Give me a couple of seconds to get my sandals on, et cetera."

"No problem." She climbed out the back, brushed herself off, and started for Chrys's tent. Once the back door snapped closed, I went about finding my sandals, straightening up, brushing my hair. When I stepped out into the heat, Chrys and Mel were waiting for me. Chrys looked a little pale.

Mel put her hands on her hips and said, as if reprimanding me, "I can't believe you didn't tell her who your brother is!"

Chrys said, "Your brother is Splay? Really?"

"Are you impressed?" I put my hand on the small of her back, and the three of us headed into the flowing line of people, all of whom seemed to be moving toward the center of the circle. We walked three abreast. I asked Mel, "How'd you know where to find us?"

"We have our agents," she said.

Chrys laughed much too loudly.

I said, "Jesus, Chrys. It wasn't that funny."

Chrys said, "I guess I'm a little nervous." Then she added, emphatically, "He didn't *look* like Splay! I mean, I'd have never guessed it, and I've probably only seen him like a billion times."

Mel said, "You can't see shit at a concert. And MTV's all makeup." She put her arm around Chrys and gave her a hug. "Believe me," she said. "He's Splay. He likes you too—as was probably obvious." She laughed girlishly, almost giggled.

The rest of the way to the trailer, Chrys and Mel walked arm in arm, chattering. I fell back a step, glad to be left out of the conversation, which was all about Splay and concerts and other rock celebrities. By the time we reached the trailer, I was feeling a little surly.

I pointed as we approached a trailer the size of a semi, twice as big as anything nearby. "Splay's playhouse on the road," I said, attempting an impression of an announcer from an old show about the rich and famous. Neither Chrys nor Mel noticed the attempt.

"This is it," Mel said, and she led us up a small metal stoop. Chrys and I waited as she unlocked the door. I was a step down from Chrys. I touched her on the thigh, gently, patting her, really. She gave me a pleasant smile. I'm sure she meant the smile to be friendly, but I bristled at it. It was the kind of smile you give someone when your mind is on something else.

Mel opened the door and guided us into an attractively furnished living room that looked more appropriate to a house than a trailer. Once the door closed, it was quiet inside. The air was still and cool, almost chilly.

"Nice," I said. "Some trailer."

"Mobile home," Mel corrected. "We spend a lot of time here." She pointed down a narrow corridor. "Why don't you go get Johnny? He might still be sleeping." She put her arm around Chrys as if they had been friends for a lifetime. "Chrys and I will find something to eat." Side by side, they looked like mother and daughter—and in the trailer light it was clear there were more than enough years between them for that to be possible. Alongside Mel, Chrys looked like a baby. The skin of her cheeks had the rosy glow of baby fat, while Mel's skin looked pulled and tucked, as if it had seen a surgical procedure or two.

On the way to the corridor, I passed a window. The trailer was situated with a perfect view of the burning man, who loomed up in the center of the circle with his arms raised, as if to embrace all his children. The window was directly over a tall table, and I stopped for a moment and took in the view of the burning man and the scores of people milling around his feet. I found it amusing that even in as artistic and anarchistic a gathering as this festival, money and fame obviously bought you some privileges—like a front-row view of the festivities. I closed my eyes and tried to gather myself. I tried to empty myself of the anger I was feeling toward Johnny. He was my brother. I had asked to see him, not the other way around. If the fact of his wealth and celebrity made Chrys behave as if she were about to meet God—that wasn't Johnny's fault. I took a deep breath and let it out slowly. From another room, one I guessed was the kitchen, I heard Chrys and Mel chattering over the clatter of dishes as drawers opened and closed. Directly across from me was another window over a table and bench set, and through that window I could see a parade of figures costumed in long flowing robes with cowls, marching toward the center of the circle. I watched them a while and then shook myself off, casting away the bad feelings.

I found Johnny in his bedroom, standing alongside an unmade bed. He was dressed in a white robe over black pajamas. He was looking into the palm of his open hand, in which there were three multicolored pills. He saw me a second after I entered the room, and he popped the three pills into his mouth, and then washed them down with a glass of water that was waiting on a bedside table. For a moment I was pissed. Then I decided, fine, maybe he'll get stoned enough to make an ass out of himself in front of Chrys.

"Kevin. Christ, man . . . ," he said. "Look at you!" He was smiling. "You've gotten old!" He crossed the room and gave me a hug, which I returned, tentatively. He felt frail in my arms, bones wrapped in skin.

I pulled back and said, "You're looking a bit thin, brother." I held his jaw in my hand. "A bit pinched and tight in the cheeks." I made a face that asked *Are you okay?*

"Too much drug and booze." He smiled wryly, patted me on the shoulder, and walked past me toward the living room.

Mel and Chrys were waiting in a booth. They had dishes of food and wicker baskets of snacks spread around. Four frosty bottles of beer marked our places. I slid behind one bottle, alongside Chrys. Splay slid in next to Mel and downed half his beer in one long gulp. Mel gave him a look, which he ignored.

Chrys said, "I still can't believe you're Splay," and she put on this coy, cute expression I hadn't seen on her before. She said, "I mean, I know, now that I know— I can see— But— *Splay*'s, like, an image— You *represent* rock or something— It's just— I can't believe you're really Splay, sitting here like this."

Johnny and Mel seemed thoroughly entertained by Chrys. Johnny said, "Want me to prove it?" and he opened his robe and started to pull apart the fly of his pajamas.

Mel slapped his hand. "Stop it," she said, and she and Chrys laughed.

I said, "That's not really true? Is it? What you're supposed to have done to your—"

"My dick?" He looked as though he couldn't believe I was asking the question. "Where do think *Splay* comes from? That's the whole—"

"I thought it was all tabloid. You really did that?" Then all three of them were looking at me as if I were out of my mind. I knew Johnny was supposed to have had an operation on his penis, that he was supposed to have had it splayed, cut along the mid-line so that the head fanned out to either side—which, I had read, was what Australian aboriginals did in some sort of ritual ceremonial thing. But I had never believed Johnny had it done. I thought it was all more of the same old rock-and-roll hype and hysteria. I didn't think he was crazy enough to do such a thing.

Johnny said, "It's historic, Kevin."

Chrys said, "Didn't someone do a PhD dissertation about it?"

Johnny said, "A kid from Rutgers."

Mel said, "He was ridiculous. The Rutgers guy. You wouldn't believe his analysis. You wouldn't believe the significance he finds in Johnny getting his dick cut."

Chrys said, adopting that terribly cute demeanor again, "I was just wondering . . ." She looked away from Johnny to Mel. "Is it true that it's . . ."

Johnny grinned and Mel looked sly and smug. I was disgusted, but did my best to hide it. I knew what Chrys was asking. According to the news stories, the splaying operation was supposed to enhance the sexual pleasure of both parties, but especially the woman's pleasure.

Mel said, still with the sly look, "We should probably all get high to talk about that." She climbed over Johnny and disappeared back into the bedroom.

I asked Chrys, "Do you get high? I mean, do you want to do this?"

Chrys just gave me a look, as if the question was too silly to answer.

Johnny said, "We got some first-rate weed, special stuff. You get high, don't you, Kevin?"

"Occasionally," I said, not telling him the last occasion was about ten years ago.

Mel climbed back to her place, and I noticed she had changed into a pair of velvety red slippers. She dropped one fat spliff on the table and lifted another to her lips. She lit up, toked, and passed it to Chrys. When Chrys handed it to me, I inhaled only a small quantity of smoke, afraid I might embarrass myself by going into a coughing fit.

Chrys said to Johnny, "Did you and Fey Wrey really have sex on stage like that? I mean, it looked like it—but no one ever really, you know, documented it . . . got a definite shot."

Johnny leaned over the table and wrapped his hands around Chrys's hands. "I'm straight," he said. "Always have been."

Mel said, "Publicity coup. Act of genius."

When Mel passed me the spliff again, I took a long toke and immediately felt darkness closing in around the edges of my vision. I tried to shake it off. I felt deliciously sleepy.

Johnny turned to Mel, still holding Chrys's hands, and said, "You know what I remember best about that night? That's the night you talked me into technology stocks."

"That was years before they went through the roof." Mel

leaned over and kissed him on the cheek. "You're welcome." To Chrys, she said, "The real genius was getting him out at the right time."

"Mel's my CEO," Johnny said. "CEO of Splay Industries. She makes seven figures a year in salary alone. She's got an MBA from . . . where?"

"Wharton." Mel flashed me a bright smile.

The conversation stalled for a moment, and then Chrys asked, "Is Fey Wrey as crazy as everyone says?"

Johnny shook his head, appearing a little annoyed at the question, as if he was tiring of Chrys's naïveté. "You know what Fey and I talk about when we get together?"

"Commodities," Mel said. She looked at Chrys. "Bore you to death."

Chrys said to Johnny, "You and Fey Wrey talk about the stock market when you get together?" She looked down at the table a moment and then started giggling convulsively.

"Jesus," I said, "what is in this weed? I can't keep my eyes open."

Johnny said, "You're getting old, brother."

Mel lit up the second spliff. "I think it's laced with some designer crap. Winston gave it to us."

Chrys said, "Winston from—"

"The same," Mel said, and passed her the new spliff.

Chrys said to Johnny, "I've always been curious about the Rats Sing video. Did you really mutilate yourself when they were taping? The part where you drag the razor across your chest?"

Johnny nodded. "I'm into that stuff," he said. "That's all true."

"What stuff?" I said. "I missed this."

"S and M," Mel said. "We're both into it." She smiled, the same lovely hostess smile she'd had going all day.

I laughed, because I didn't know what to say.

Johnny said, "What's the matter, brother? You shocked by my sexual proclivities?"

"You're serious?" I said.

Johnny looked angry for a moment. "How can you know so little about me, Kevin? Chrys here knows more about me—and you're my brother."

"Johnny," I said, "I still don't know whether you're putting me on or not. Really, in real life, you're into S and M?"

Johnny shook his head and laughed and looked away, like I was just too much of a dolt for him to deal with.

Mel said, "It's a sexual preference. It's not that big a deal."

I was high at this point, but it was a weird, sleepy high. I felt so exhausted I couldn't keep my thoughts straight, the way I might get in the few moments before I go under to sleep. I think I might have been slurring my words. "So you, like, what," I said, "whip each other? That kind of thing?"

"Oh for God's sake," Chrys said, as if coming to Johnny and Mel's defense, "the whole culture gets off sexually on violence. S and M is just straight up about it."

"The whole culture gets off sexually on violence?" I looked at Chrys as if she had to be kidding. "You don't think that's just a little glib?"

Johnny said, "Brother, you're being a jerk. Go to the movies. The more violent it is, the longer the line out the door."

"I wouldn't argue that," I said, and I was amazed at how coherent I sounded, given I felt like I was talking underwater. "It's the sexual response to violence I have trouble with."

All three of them looked at me in silence, as if I were the village idiot and they were stunned by the extent of my stupidity. Finally,

Chrys said, "You've got trouble with it?" She frowned. Then she added, suggestively, "That's *really* too bad."

"Why?" I asked, because I didn't get what she was saying.

Chrys looked at me as if I were hopeless. Then she looked at Johnny and Mel and the three of them broke into laughter.

After a moment, I laughed along with them, as if I too were amazed at my naïveté. "Oh," I said to Chrys, finally getting it. "You too, huh?" I dropped my head on the table and said, "You know what? This weed is making me stupid and tired. Great stuff."

Johnny said, "You always were a little slow on the uptake, Kevin."

"Thank you," I said, and I think I sounded as if I wasn't at all pissed off and a little humiliated. "You guys mind if I just go to sleep here?"

Johnny said, "Try this." He went to the table and benches opposite us, and with a couple of movements, he dropped the table and pushed the benches together so they formed a bed, mattress and all. I must have been wrecked—whatever was in that spliff, it was nothing like regular weed. The way he turned the benches into a bed looked like a magic trick to me. When I said, "How did you do that?" everyone laughed.

I was the local clown, happy to amuse the three of them.

Johnny said, "Knock yourself out, Kevin."

I wasn't sure what he meant, but the bed looked like a piece of paradise to me. I dragged myself over to it and dropped onto the mattress. I closed my eyes with something like orgasmic pleasure. The last thing I remember was hearing Chrys and Mel talking, and then Mel telling Johnny to pull the curtain for me, and opening my eyes long enough to see Johnny pulling a curtain around me, turning what had been a table and benches into a small bedroom.

I remember thinking the words *mobile home*, and then cuddling up into the mattress and giving myself over to sleep.

When I opened my eyes it was dark. From beyond the trailer walls I heard music and the sublittoral drone of water, water rolling in waves against sand and rocks—until I remembered where I was, and then the sound of waves turned into voices of the crowd shouting and screaming. I tried to sit up, thinking, from the noise, that I must be missing the burning, but my head felt heavy, and I didn't move, and I think I must have fallen asleep again because the next time I opened my eyes the noise had abated, though I could still hear occasional shouting and music. My head felt better, and after I lay still awhile longer, my thoughts cleared and I remembered exactly where I was and what was going on. I sat up slowly and when I opened the curtain, I found myself looking at the empty booth, where I had left Johnny and Chrys and Mel. On the table was a burnt spoon and a syringe next to a spill of dark liquid in the middle of which were a couple of soggy roaches.

I threw my legs over the edge of my little bed and sat a moment in the dark, and then Johnny came out of the bedroom and turned on the lights. When he saw me, he said, "Feeling better?" He took a seat across from me.

"What's going on?" I asked. "Where's Chrys?"

He gestured toward the bedroom. "She's more than a little crazy," he said. "She's in there with Mel."

I laughed and rubbed my eyes. Johnny's robe had fallen open at the top, and I could see the outline of his body clearly beneath his silky pajamas. He was so thin, he looked like a skeleton. He looked ghastly to me, a rack of bones.

Beyond him, through the window, I could see the figure

of the burning man, a few flames still playing along the torso and head. I looked back at the closed bedroom door. "All these years I haven't seen you," I said, "and all you can think to do is humiliate me."

Johnny made a face, as if to say it wasn't like that. "I didn't do anything," he said. "It's Chrys and Mel in there. I didn't do a damn thing."

"Johnny," I said. "I just saw you walk out of the bedroom."

"Okay," he said, and he shrugged. "So I watched."

I stood up. "So fuck you," I said. I walked out of the trailer.

Outside, on the steps, I hesitated a moment before heading off into the dirt and heat. I'm not sure what I was feeling as I walked away: relief, sadness . . . emptiness mostly, I think. Nothing, with sadness and anger hovering around the edges. I walked. The burning man had burned. There were lots of people around, crowds and throngs of people looking excited or tired, pumped up or crashing. Many in costumes. I wasn't paying a lot of attention. I walked toward the burning man, and when I came upon two empty lawn chairs inside a drawn circle on the cracked desert sand, I stepped into the circle and took a seat. There was no one in the immediate vicinity: it was a shadowy spot ten feet beyond a ring of tents and parachute structures, where a couple must have gotten away from their friends to watch the burning. I didn't think they'd mind if I rested a while. I looked up, and as I did, one of the burning man's arms fell to the ground and exploded in a bright splash of red embers. People roared their approval. Then Johnny stepped into the circle and sat alongside me. He fell down heavily into the chair, as if exhausted, and he looked at me a long moment without speaking. He reminded me for a minute of the Johnny I remembered as a kid, my older brother, the guy I always turned to when I did something stupid.

I said, "You followed me?"

"I was going to wring your neck," he said, "before I remembered I couldn't wring a puppy's neck, let alone a big old guy like you." He added, "How'd you get so old, Kevin?"

I sat up in my chair and leaned over to look more closely at him. He was sweating and pale. If I wasn't so fed up with him, I'd have been worried. "What the hell's wrong with you, Johnny? Don't tell me you have AIDS," I said. "Or is it just the drugs?"

"What drugs?"

"I don't know," I said, "Start with the ones I saw you popping in the bedroom."

"Those were meds, Sherlock. I take medications every four and six hours."

I waited, prompting him to explain.

"I don't have AIDS," he said. "What I've got is kidneys that are near gone, a liver that's a wreck, and last year I had a stroke. Sometimes I can barely talk."

I leaned back in the lawn chair, away from Johnny, and then I looked away.

He added, "I'm around another year, it'll be a gift."

I didn't know what to say. I rubbed my forehead hard with the heel of my hand. Fact was, even finding out all this, I was still disgusted with him. He must have been able to feel it.

He said, "What do you want from me, Kevin? Do I disappoint you? Am I a problem? Have I disturbed your pleasant life?"

"How could I have a pleasant life," I said, "with you as my brother?"

"And what can I do about that?" he said. "Way it is." He was quiet awhile, and then he laughed a small, quiet laugh that went on and on.

I was silent. I had nothing to say. When Johnny finally managed to stop laughing, he leaned toward me and put his hand on my forearm. His fingers were dry and rough, like an old man's, and I was surprised at the feel of it, my brother's hand. I put my hand over his. Above us, the night sky darkened. Around us, the noise of the crowd diminished. Together we remained there like that, with his hand on my arm and my hand over his hand—brothers, looking up at the black husk of the burning man, the charred figure, wrecked and smoldering.

Candy

Forty-four years from then, Terry would be retired, living on Sea Island in Georgia, spending most of his time playing golf, reading, doing this and that with his wife, or visiting his children—but then he was in the back of a van with eight drunks, on his way to Monticello, a resort town in the Catskills. He was working for a friend with whom he had gone to college at Cornell, and who was in turn working as the manager of Monticello Employment Force, an agency that supplied labor for the various conventions and trade shows that went on in the Catskills. His friend, Marcus, was up front, driving. Also up front, where Terry should have been, was an old guy everyone called Candy because his real name was a string of unpronounceable Polish syllables. In the back with Terry were Arney, Edwin, Adam, Buster, Eugene, Jimmy, Hugh, and Zack. He knew them all from prior drunk-runs to The Bowery, where he'd cruise the streets looking for familiar faces—though, usually, he wouldn't even have to look. Marcus would drive along slowly until he saw someone pull himself up off the sidewalk and step to the curb, as if his bus had finally arrived. He'd pull over and Terry would get out, open the back door, close it behind whichever drunk it was ready to work for a few days, and then get back in up front beside Marcus and continue cruising until the van was full. But Terry had never ridden in the back before, and the stink—with an hour yet before Monticello—was making him sick.

Eugene, seated cross-legged on the carpeted floor of the van directly across from Terry, was muttering to himself, his head nodding in a state that suggested either exhaustion or insanity. Everyone else, with the exception of Buster, was sleeping or pretending to sleep. Buster was situated with his back against the cab, staring out the rear windows.

"What are you doing back here?" Eugene asked, suddenly, and with a full twist of hostility, as if he had just noticed Terry and was pissed off at the sight of him. Terry didn't bother to answer. He knew better than to talk to an angry drunk. Instead, he pulled himself to his knees, steadied himself by the rear doors, and then opened one door a crack to let some air in. The smell, an acrid mix of bodily waste, sweat, and whiskey, was killing him. The usual routine was to dump these guys off at the convention hotel, get them settled in rooms, and then give them a free day to get sober and cleaned up before putting them to work. Most of them were good at their jobs. They'd work hard for three or four days, putting in sometimes eighteen or twenty hours a day, until the convention floor was set up and ready to go. Then they'd go back to the city and drink up what they earned. This crew, though, this run— Terry pulled his nose out of the crack in the door and looked behind him at the battered and bedraggled sprawled over the floor of the van. This crew looked like they might need more than a day.

Behind him, Buster said, sounding utterly sober, "Close the damn door, kid. You're making me nervous."

Candy

"What do you think?" Eugene said, his voice gravelly and thick. "You think he's jumpin' out or somethin'?"

Terry closed the door and settled back against the wall of the van.

Eugene said, "I ast you why you're back here. You didn't hear me?" He leaned forward. Eugene was a bearded guy Terry knew to be in his thirties from the records at the agency, but he looked like he should be at least fifty, maybe older. His skin, what you could see of it, was deeply lined with wrinkles and marked with cuts and scrapes. His eyes were bloodshot, and on both eyelids he had tiny cysts or pimples of some sort. His teeth were mossy and yellow, and even across the van Terry could smell the stink of his breath.

When Terry didn't answer, Eugene said, louder, "You ignoring me?"

Buster, without taking his eyes off the windows, said, "Shut up, Eugene, or I'll come over there and throw you out of the van."

"Yeah you will," Eugene said. Then he added, sounding as if he were talking to himself, "I'm not doing nothing. What's the kid doing back here, is all."

Terry said, "Candy wouldn't come unless he got to ride in the cab."

Buster laughed quietly, and Eugene said, childish and mocking, "Oh Candy Candy, Mr. Big Shit. Candy Candy Candy."

Candy was a cook, which was a position much more in demand than the commonplace manual laborer. He had spent the summer season in the Catskills every year from long before Terry knew anything about the place. Word was the two big hotels, the Concord and Grossinger's, vied for his services. He'd run the kitchen where he worked with expertise and efficiency until the summer season was over, and then he'd go back to the city for the rest of the year, where, word was, he had his own apartment. Candy was a drunk, but he was a different order of drunk from the homeless, the soup-kitchen, sleep-on-the-street drunks. He didn't look terribly beat-up, though he wasn't in good shape either. He was a wiry thin man, in his mid-sixties, with lanky arms and long fingers, a beakish nose and a full head of white hair, which he wore slicked straight back. He was handsome in a distant, intellectual way, though his face, too, bore the scrapes and eruptions of hard drinking.

Given that Candy usually just appeared in one of the hotels once the summer season started, Terry had been surprised when he saw him walk out to the curb, a small suitcase in hand, as the van approached. Marcus had been driving slowly, hovering close to the sidewalk, and Terry had been leaning out his window, trying to discern a familiar face among the drunks lined up against buildings, sitting in clusters or stretched out sleeping. It was late May. Not yet 7 A.M. The agency liked the van to get there early to give the guys a night's sleep head start on the sobering-up process. Candy had hobbled out to the curb looking surprisingly beat-up, looking almost like one of the street drunks on the sidewalks, on fire escapes, in doorways throughout the neighborhood. Still, his scarecrow frame and slicked-back white hair made him recognizable. Once Marcus pulled over and stopped, Terry hopped out of his seat and scurried to the curb, all smiles, expecting a warm greeting. He knew Candy from the two previous summers, when he had spent several weeks working at Grossinger's, where Candy was the cook. He had imagined a kind of camaraderie between them. Neither were really hotel workers. Terry had aspirations as an artist, a painter. He had a few small canvases tucked away in his tiny dorm room at Grossinger's. His degree from Cornell had been in communications, but his heart wasn't into pursuing a comfortable career. Candy was a pianist, or had been until, Terry assumed, drink took it away from him. What Terry knew about Candy—and it wasn't much—came from others. Candy didn't talk about himself. He adopted a paternal attitude toward all the young workers at Grossinger's, including Terry. He was smart, that much was clear simply from the way he spoke, but he also had a kind of warmth that drew other people to him. So when Terry trotted over to greet him, he was surprised when Candy spoke to him and looked at him like every other drunk they picked up off the street.

"I'm not coming," Candy said, "unless I sit in the front of the fuckin' van. Okay? You ride in back with the animals." He was drunk. Terry could smell it on him, and he heard it in his attitude—that belligerence typical of drunks.

"Sure," he said, and he had tried to laugh off the hostility.

Candy had nodded to him, a little angry nod of gratitude.

Now, in the back of the van, Terry wasn't regretting his choice so much as suffering with it. The smell . . . The smell was nearly unbearable, a mix of a sewer, a distillery, and a locker room. He wondered what Buster had going for him, sitting there with his back against the cab, looking out the rear windows as if he were relaxing in the cushy seating of an air-conditioned theater.

Terry said, "Hey, Buster," thinking to ask him what was so interesting about this boring stretch of the New York State Thruway. Buster, though, ignored him. When Eugene snickered, Terry leaned against the wall of the van, closed his eyes, and waited patiently for the ride to come to an end.

• • •

Burning Man

Terry had retired at age sixty-five from a forty-year career at the *Washington Post*, as a reporter and then an editor, but it was only recently, at sixty-eight, that he felt he had fully left behind that other life in D.C. His wife, who had been a four-term congresswoman from New Jersey, had, in his opinion, still not retired. Her daily thoughts were full of politics, she read several newspapers each morning, and she was on a dozen boards and committees. For the first year or so after retirement, things had been much the same for Terry, but in the last couple of years he had found his interest in such things waning. Now he preferred to play golf in the morning, nap in the afternoon, and spend his evenings out on the deck reading and looking off at the endless variety of weather over the ocean, especially the spring and summer thunderstorms, with their lightning displays playing out over a merged line of sea and sky. On the deck, lately, at night, his thoughts kept returning to those three years between finishing up at Cornell and starting a career in D.C., the years when he lived in the Catskills and worked hotel jobs during the day and mostly just hung out drinking and fooling around with friends and girlfriends at night. He was into gambling a little on the horses, and into poker at night in the hotels with workers mostly, but sometimes guests too. He was really into girls, girls he'd meet through the hotel, both guests and workers, and a few girls from in town, though there weren't many of those. They were years of dreams too, dreams of being an artist.

The tricks of memory are fascinating. His career, most of his life, felt like one fast blur of time, as if he were hired at the *Post* one day as a skinny, single kid, and retired the next, fat, with a family and full life history. His memory was good—it wasn't as if he couldn't remember the years of career and family—but the

Candy

memories from those three years in the Catskills were vivid, were electric when he settled into them, when he replayed them as if he were looking for something. The memory of Candy that morning in late May, of the ride back in the van, was sharp and precise, alive with detail and feeling. When they arrived in Monticello, Terry had tumbled out of the back of the van and dragged himself to the cab, where he collapsed against the passenger window as if he were dying, his eyes bugged out, his mouth open—cracking up both Marcus and Candy. Candy had put his hand on Terry's head and said, gently, "I owe you."

Terry could still see himself in that moment, draped over the passenger window in faded blue jeans and a crisp white T, sandals and longish, thick black hair, a handsome kid, a little taller than average, in the best physical shape of his life from regular manual labor. He wore white T-shirts all the time because he liked the way they accented his biceps, which had grown impressive from unloading trucks at the convention sites. He also thought of it as a signature look—the kid with the thick black hair who always wore white T's. And when he dripped paint on his jeans, that was fine, that was like a signature too. When he got around to it, he painted barefoot and bare chested in his tiny room, or sometimes with an easel, out in the woods or by the lake or around town. He had a reputation in Monticello as the young artist who worked in the hotels. For a while he was with a beautiful girl, Viola, who was employed as a stripper at a bar across from the raceway. She was eighteen, just out of high school, and beautiful if not especially bright—but nice, and he loved the way she was proud of him and believed in him and loved everything he said. Though he always knew it wouldn't be permanent with Vi, he told her he loved her, which he did in a way, and he didn't actively discourage her obvious hopes for a permanent relationship—though he never thought of her as someone he might marry.

Late nights he'd often go to the club to watch Vi dance, and a few nights after the Candy bum-run, he was at a table with a bunch of waiters from Grossinger's and the Concord. It wasn't late, maybe ten o'clock, ten thirty, when one of the big shots from the Concord walked into the club with a half dozen guys in suits. The club was long and wide, with high ceilings. It was a warehouse of a place with a bar and a stage against the back wall, a runway in the middle of the bar extending into the tables that occupied the center of the room. Dozens of booths lined the walls. Above the runway on both walls were private balcony seats and the VIP room, which Terry had never seen. The big shot, whom Terry barely knew, recognized a couple of his waiters and nodded in their direction before disappearing up the stairs to the balcony.

Terry found a spot open at the bar where it met the runway, and ordered another bourbon and coke. He'd had a couple already and was beginning to feel the euphoric rush of sensation and emotion that came with getting drunk. Ann Marie, a friend of Vi's, was finishing up her set. She winked at him as she strutted along the runway naked, having taken four songs to remove the last of her schoolgirl getup, from the uniform white blouse and pleated plaid skirt, down to the bobby socks and patent leather shoes. On either side of the runway, men were whistling and clapping as her song came to an end and she strutted a little half-dance past the packed tables with men leaning close to the runway edge to get one last good look at her. Terry knew that Ann Marie was twenty-one—he had gone out drinking with her and Vi and a half dozen others for her birthday a few weeks earlier—but she looked like a baby. She looked like she couldn't be more than sixteen.

She was thin and small-breasted, unlike the typical Playboy-bunny body, but she was almost always the biggest hit of the evening. When she danced, men would line up at the edges of the runway like supplicants at the altar.

The bartender handed Terry his drink just as Ann Marie was coming off the runway, and the pounding music she had been dancing to came to an abrupt stop, signaling the end of the clapping and hooting. On her way past Terry, before disappearing through a curtain and into the back rooms, she stopped, knelt in front of him, removed the bourbon and coke playfully from his hand and winked at him as she took a sip. Behind her, Vi came through the curtain in her western outfit—fringed vest, chaps, boots, hat, the whole cowboy cliché. She was smiling until she saw Ann Marie sipping Terry's drink; then the smile disappeared and gave way to a look of momentary surprise followed by a glare as she met Terry's eyes. Terry shrugged as if to say *I didn't do anything*. Ann Marie looked back at Vi, smiled at her, and sauntered off the opposite end of the stage. By the time the kitschy cowboy music started up and Vi loped onto the stage twirling her tiny lasso, Terry was halfway back to his table and Vi appeared to be caught up in her act. He suspected, though, he'd hear about Ann Marie later. He'd think about what to say when he took his spot sitting on the back door railing, waiting for Vi to finish up for the night.

At his table, he found a waitress delivering another round of drinks for everyone. She placed a bourbon and coke on a coaster in front of him as he retook his seat. The big shot from the Concord had apparently decided to slum a bit with his waiters, and he was holding forth to their rapt attention as Terry joined them. The guy was short and heavy, but compact, with broad shoulders. It looked like it would take a tank to knock him down. He was dressed in a dark blue striped three-piece suit, with a bright yellow tie bowed out awkwardly over the top of his vest. He was at the end of a story about a waiter from last summer who had climbed out the window of a guest's room naked when her husband came back unexpectedly early from a round of golf. The waiter had his clothes tucked under one arm as he scrambled precariously along the roof on his way to the fire escape, where he'd have enough room to sit down and get dressed. "A plan," the big shot said, "that might have worked if there hadn't happened to be a Bat Mitzvah going on in the courtyard." The waiters at the table, all of whom had heard the story a hundred times, cracked up as if hearing it for the first time. The big shot shook his head sorrowfully and said, "Had to fire him," for a few more laughs. He looked at Terry and added, "You're working for Marcus, right? Did you hear about Buster?"

"No," Terry said. "Something happen?"

"In the county jail," he said. "Got caught in a guest's room going through luggage."

"Shit," Terry said, "wouldn't have guessed him." He finished his drink and started on the fresh one. "Thanks," he said, toasting the guy before he took a sip.

"I'm Mort," he said, announcing his name in response to the toast. Then he added, "You got to watch all those guys. You can't trust any of them."

"Christ," Terry said, agreeing with him. "I drove up in the back of the van with a load of them last week? I had to burn my clothes." When the table laughed, he added, "I hear Eugene took three days sleeping it off before he was worth shit working."

Mort said, "I heard about that. You let Candy ride up front?" He flagged down a passing waitress and ordered another drink

Candy

for Terry. When Terry tried to protest, Mort said, "It's from Candy, via me." Then he got up, bowed to the table dramatically, and headed back up to the balcony.

One of the waiters said, "Those guys all love Candy. It's like he walks on water with them or something."

Another waiter added, "He used to be, like, some kind of big deal classical pianist, like a hundred years ago."

"Get out of here," someone else said.

"Seriously," the waiter insisted. "I've seen CDs with him at the piano on the cover. It was the New York Philharmonic or some big deal orchestra like that."

"Candy?" Terry said.

"I'm telling you," the waiter said. "I saw the CD."

"That's fucked up," someone else said, and then they all looked over to the runway as Vi peeled off the last of her outfit and started dancing around a white cowboy hat.

The waiter sitting next to Terry turned to him and said, "Dude, you are one lucky son of a bitch."

Terry flashed him a wicked smile, as if to say *You don't know the half of it*, and then looked at his watch as Vi pranced off the stage with her music fading and the house giving her a loud round of applause. It was only 11:30, which meant another two and a half hours before Vi was off and he could pick her up and go back to her place. He finished his drink, pulled himself up out of his seat, and took his leave of the table.

Outside, in front of the club, he looked warily at his car, a beat-up rust red Volvo he'd been driving since his senior year in college without ever bothering with as much as an oil change. It always amazed him that it continued to run with hardly a complaint. For a moment he considered that he was obviously drunk and shouldn't drive, but he quickly pushed aside his qualms, telling himself there was never anybody on the road, and it was a short drive to Grossinger's, where he planned on going to find Candy. It had occurred to him at the table that Candy would have something to say about art and being an artist that would be worth hearing, and he had decided on the spot to find him and ask—though precisely what he was going to ask was not clear, was in fact bubbly and effervescent, an unformed half question, something on the order of "What's art all about, Candy?" though, sitting behind the wheel of his Volvo, contemplating turning the ignition key, Terry thought what he really wanted to know was whether or not he, Terry, was an artist—and how in hell could Candy or anyone else answer that question for him? So what was he doing, going to find Candy? Terry looked out the high front window of the Volvo to a dark sky full of stars and decided he felt good about going to find Candy and that he'd trust his feelings, even if he didn't know what the hell he would ask him if he found him. He knew where the kitchen was at Grossinger's. He knew where the kitchen staff were housed. That was a start.

On the road out of Monticello, he drove slowly and paid careful attention to the white lines on the pavement, which the car seemed to have a tendency to want to cross over. He had decided—wisely, he complimented himself—to take the back roads to Grossinger's. The night was gorgeous, and once out of Monticello, traveling narrow two-lane roads surrounded by rolling farmland, the sky zoomed in closer, alive with bright stars and inky black space. When he came upon a field with cows lined up against a wire fence, he slowed the car, stopped and turned off his lights, and rolled down his window to look back at the big, slow beasts lining the road. His head was buzzing, and when he opened the car door to get out, the world swirled around him. He laughed at his drunkenness and said to the cows, "I'm drunk, girls," and then laughed some more before leaning over a slight ditch between the field and the road, unzipping, and peeing on the ditch grass. In front of him, a pair of cows shook their shoulders and one of them mooed. Terry mooed back, eliciting a small rustling in the herd, as if he were beginning to annoy them. "Sorry, girls," he said. He got back in his car and then sat there awhile in the quiet, breathing deeply as he looked out the windows at the night and the sky, waiting to sober up so that he wouldn't make a fool out of himself when he found Candy and tried to ask him whatever the question was he wanted to ask.

Terry had been thinking about doing an oil painting of a dilapidated half-caved-in barn he'd come across outside of town. He had at least some natural talent, he thought, because he found it easy to paint a scene as he saw it. He was good at getting the perspective and the colors right, so that with a little concentration and enough time he could usually get an impressive likeness of a scene down on canvas. That was no little thing, he told himself, to be able to paint the world as he saw it, to be able to capture a little piece of the world and preserve it in a painting. He knew, of course, that landscape painting had been long out of vogue, that contemporary artists were mixing up painting and sculpture and photography and even dance; that they were interested now in work that played on the boundaries between life and art. He had taken a couple of courses at Cornell on art and culture, so he wasn't a primitive; he wasn't someone who went at what he was doing with no idea. But he had zero interest in abstraction: when he tried it, he felt nothing. He had no interest in painting on fabric, or reproducing comic strips or Brillo boxes. He had no interest

Burning Man

in mixing up mediums, and he didn't even really fully understand what was meant by "conceptual" art. He had a talent for painting scenes that looked lovely to him, like falling-down barns or like this night sky spread out so gorgeously before him. He wanted to paint beautiful and lovely things, and he didn't see why that shouldn't be valuable. Why should a print of a Campbell's soup can be more important than a painting of the ocean in moonlight? Really.

That, he decided, was the question he would ask Candy. Why couldn't he just paint beautiful scenes? What was wrong with that? He started the Volvo, hit the gas, and inadvertently sprayed the herd of cows at the fence line with gravel and dust. He whispered an apology to them as the Volvo sped along the road toward Grossinger's.

On Sea Island, on his deck, Terry hauled himself up out of his lounge chair. He went back into the house and searched through his music collection until he found the CD with Candy on the cover, seated behind an elegant grand piano, an orchestra blurry in the background. He took the CD with him back out to the deck and examined it as he leaned over the railing. The sea, a hundred feet in front of him, was still and glassy under a bright moon. The sky was clear, a glittery array of stars only here and there obscured by drifting clouds. The man behind the piano on the CD cover was obviously Candy: same nose, same deep eyes, even the same hairstyle, slicked back, only darker hair and thicker than when Terry knew him. He was still a young man at the time of the recording, but his eyes were the same, and he wore his typical expression, as if some part of him were always a million miles away and he was looking out at the world across that long distance.

When Terry found Candy that night, the night of the cows and the drinking, he was sitting alone in the kitchen, wearing new clothes—gray slacks and a dark shirt, shiny black shoes and a lightweight fall jacket. He looked more like one of the guests than a kitchen worker—but his face was still beat-up, with a few scrapes on his cheek, and a scabbed cut high on his temple. He greeted Candy cheerfully, as if happily surprised at having crossed paths with him, but Candy wasn't the same guy from the previous summers. That guy would have smiled and said something reassuring. This Candy asked Terry what he was doing in the kitchen after midnight.

"What are you doing here?" Terry said, coming back at Candy a little, bolstered by the drink still in his system. He wasn't sloppy drunk, but he was still high.

"What? Did your girlfriend toss you out?" Candy dragged himself to his feet. He looked as though he had been working hard all day and was tired. "Mr. Terry," he added, a little less surly, "What are you doing in my kitchen?"

"Looking for you," Terry said. He shoved his hands in his pockets and grinned at Candy. "I have a question for you about art."

Candy found a set of keys on a stainless steel countertop, and he put them in his pocket. "And you expected to find me in the kitchen at this hour?"

"I know you can't sleep," he said. "I thought I'd check here first and then the dorms."

Candy laughed at that. "You were going to come to my room after midnight," he said, sounding as if he were talking to himself. He put his hand on Terry's arm as he walked past him, on the way to the swinging doors that led out to the dining room. "You can walk back with me," he said, "and ask me your question." He held a door open for Terry. "But don't ever again come looking for me when you're drunk. You understand that?"

"Sure," Terry said. "I'm not that drunk."

Candy started making his way around the covered tables artfully arranged throughout the dining room, and Terry followed him. When they reached the other side of the room, he said, "Sorry, Candy. But, really. I'm not that drunk."

"Fine," Candy said. "How can I help you?" He stopped, as if something had surprised him, and turned to look at Terry. "What is it you want?" he asked.

"Like I said . . ." Terry tried out a warm smile. Previous summers he'd had a dozen conversations with Candy about art and artists. It wasn't like coming to ask him a question about art was so entirely weird. For an instant it occurred to Terry that Candy didn't remember their talks, that his alcoholism might have so messed with his memory that he didn't remember much about anything. "You know," he said, "we've talked before about—"

"I know," Candy said, and started walking again, heading toward the empty lounge on his way to a side door. "You want to be an artist," he said, and then he added, "You're doing a good job with the drinking and fooling around."

"I am?" Terry said, still following.

"How's that girl from town?" Candy asked. "Viola?"

"She's fine," Terry said. "I'm picking her up from here."

"At the place where she's working as a stripper?"

Terry didn't answer. The conversation seemed to be moving forward along two different tracks, with Terry wanting to talk about one thing and Candy another. "Look," Terry said, "this is what I wanted to ask you about." They had crossed into the lounge, and

Candy's eyes were on the glistening black grand piano at the front of the room. "It'll just take a second."

Candy stopped and pulled a chair out from under a nearby table. He gestured for Terry to sit. "What? What is it you think I might have to tell you?"

Terry laughed and rubbed his forehead, trying to stall a few moments. Put on the spot, the question seemed ridiculous. "I don't know," he said, "it's going to sound stupid now."

"I don't doubt it," Candy said.

Terry looked up at him, annoyed. He wanted, suddenly, to tell him off.

Candy noticed the anger, and his voice softened. "You're not entirely contemptible yet, Terry—but you are a fraud, no?"

"Why are you being like this?" Terry said. "Did I do something?"

"You got a year older," Candy said. "What are you, twenty-four, twenty-five now?"

"What does that have to do with anything?"

"What do you want?" Candy said, sounding very tired. "I don't have all night for this."

Terry shrugged, wanting only to ask his question and get out of there. "I like painting beautiful scenes," he said, matter-of-factly. "I wondered why, you know, people don't much care about that kind of painting anymore."

Candy said, "Why would I know anything about that?"

"Because you're an artist," Terry said, "or you were."

Candy only grinned at the dig. "Someone's keeping you from painting beautiful scenes? You should paint what you want to paint."

"No one's keeping me," Terry said. "That's not the question. The question—"

"It would help if you'd lived through some more," Candy said. "*How* you saw the world, *what* you saw, might be different." Then he added, "If you'd been through more, were a different kind of person, you might think differently about what's beautiful."

Terry said, "Maybe I should have been an alcoholic."

"Or a Jew in Poland in the thirties."

"That's you?" Terry said.

Candy got up without answering and started to walk away. Then he stopped and went to the piano. "What do I know?" he said. "I don't know what you are or aren't. You want to hear something beautiful?" He fingered the keys, playing a few notes. "This is Beethoven," he said. The *Tempest* Sonata. He started to play, and at first Terry was flattered. He'd never heard Candy play, nor had he heard of anyone else who'd heard him play—and there he was, playing for him, the music starting out gently, sounding like the classical music Terry had heard before here and there, on the radio or on recordings. After a short while, though, the tempo picked up and the music grew stranger, different from what he'd heard before, and he realized the music was making him uncomfortable, though he couldn't have said why—then or later. There was something in the speed of it, in the differing volume of each note, something that imparted to the music a kind of chaotic disorder, a kind of terror, and as he watched he saw Candy had disappeared into the music. Though he sat perfectly upright at the piano, he seemed simultaneously to be hunched over it, as if his body were somehow projecting into the music and into the piano itself, which hummed and vibrated and trembled with cascading sound.

When he was finished, Candy picked himself up from the piano bench and left the room looking exhausted, without as much as a glance back at Terry.

How many times in his life had Terry's thoughts flashed back to that night? Hundreds of times? Thousands? It was as if there was something underneath the music that night, something both beautiful and disquieting. But more and different. Something he never could name that always drew him back to the memory: Candy at the piano, him at the table, that music filling up the lounge—and the sense he was in the presence of something not entirely inviting, attractive but also threatening.

For a while, Terry remained in the lounge. Rather than feeling sympathy for Candy, for what he must have gone through as a young man, being a Jew in Poland in the thirties; rather than feeling appreciation, for the years of work and study that must have been behind that performance; rather than any of that, what he felt was anger. Candy had called him a fraud, and the word crept under his skin and itched. He felt somehow as if the music itself had been a kind of attack, and the longer he sat alone in the room the more uncomfortable he became. When he finally pulled himself away from the table and went out to his car, it was with a sense of relief.

The night was still gorgeous, and he drove back slowly with the windows open, enjoying the air on his face and in his hair. By the time he got to the club, he was feeling better. He pulled into his regular spot, and took his seat on the railing of the back door stoop, and a moment later, Ann Marie came out. She was wearing glued-on blue jeans and a sheer white blouse, and she had her hair pulled back in a ponytail.

Terry said, "Hey," and offered her his brightest smile.

Ann Marie didn't say anything for a second. She looked him over, as if appraising him, and then she pulled a pen out of a red handbag slung over her shoulder, took one of his hands in hers, and wrote her phone number on his palm. "You know you want to," she said, and then she went on to her car and drove off with Terry watching. She was just out of the parking lot when Vi came through the door and kissed Terry on the cheek. "I'm sooo tired," she said. "I swear to God, one more stranger grabs my ass . . ."

Terry hopped down from the railing, put his arm around her, and squeezed her shoulder. She was dressed almost identically to Ann Marie, with tight jeans, a white blouse, and a handbag slung over her shoulder, only her handbag was black. "Another rough night?" he asked, and he settled in as she started on her nightly litany of complaints. Usually she'd go on nonstop until she got to her house, where they'd both wind down with weed and music before wrestling into bed—if they made it to the bed. That night, though, before they got to her house, Vi stopped in midsentence as she examined the sleeve of her blouse. "What the hell?"

Terry looked over, saw the blue smudge of ink on her sleeve, and knew immediately what had happened. "Oh, shit," he said. "I'm sorry." He took his hand off the wheel for half a second and flashed the ink on his palm in her direction. "I wrote a phone number down so I wouldn't forget it."

Vi frowned, still examining the ink stain on her blouse. "It'll come out," she said. "No big deal. Whose phone number?"

"Candy's," Terry said. "I was just at Grossinger's with him."

"God," she said, "really. I'm sooo tired." She stretched her legs, was quiet a moment looking out the side window, and started in again, complaining about some guy who offered her a hundred dollars to let him suck on her breasts. "You believe that?" she said.

Terry had no problem believing it. She had told him a hundred stories just like it before. "What did you tell him?"

"I told him I wasn't a prostitute," she said, which was her standard reply when guys asked for something more than a dance.

"Was he okay with it?"

Vi shrugged and then went on to the next story, about the next jerk.

At her house, which she shared with three other girls, he parked under a chestnut tree next to the driveway, and then went around back with her and up a flight of stairs that led to a private entrance into her room. She kept her key on top of the light next to the door, and when Terry reached for it, she took his hand gently by the wrist and pulled it to her. Awkwardly, Terry half closed his hand, trying to hide the number.

Vi's eyes filled with tears. "You're a liar," she said, and she took the key from him, let herself in, and closed the door behind her.

Terry left Vi's that night, found a phone, called Ann Marie, and spent the night with her. A couple of weeks later, when Ann Marie dropped him, he left the Catskills for D.C. When he moved out of his room in Monticello, he wrapped up his paintings and supplies in black plastic and left them at the dump. He had considered leaving them at Candy's door, but decided against it.

Terry found a CD player and headphones in the house. It wasn't late, maybe eleven o'clock or so, but his wife had been asleep for hours. He thought he'd listen to some Beethoven awhile and then go to bed himself. He leaned over the CD cabinet, flipping through his collection of classical music. He had a substantial belly and thick thighs these days, and his cheeks had gone jowly. He wanted to hear Beethoven's *Tempest* Sonata. He probably had more than twenty recordings of it. He picked one at random and went out to the deck. It didn't matter which recording he took, because nothing he had on CD sounded anything like the music he had heard that night in the Catskills. In his lounge chair, he lay back and closed his eyes and listened, the one pianist's lovely version of the *Tempest* Sonata playing in this world, and Candy's version, its terrors safely in the distant past, playing hauntingly beneath it.

Winter Storms

THROUGH SNOW, IN THE GRAY LIGHT OF STORM CLOUDS massing over the beach, Rick thought he saw a figure in a knee-length quilted white coat approaching him as he squinted through the furred circle of his parka hood. He pushed himself forward while wind screamed ashore skimming water off waves so that the air itself was wet and it seemed as though he was walking in water and through snow at the same time. He had taken this walk along the Fire Island beach in winter before, and he knew how the bitterly cold wind could make bare skin burn. He knew how to dress for such walks: in an arctic parka, with good boots and thermal underwear under several layers of clothes. Still, this was a test. He could barely make headway against the wind. Storm-pushed waters had reduced the wide beach to a narrow strip of sand, and visibility was failing rapidly, threatening to turn everything into an indeterminate field of gray light—and since the point of a walk like this was to see up close the rage of the ocean in a storm, he was on the verge of turning back, of turning his back against the wind and letting it push him toward the parking lot where his red Jeep waited. But he was almost sure he had seen someone in the distance, walking toward him from Fire Island, and the prospect was so improbable—that someone else would be out on the beach in a storm like this—that he pushed on, peering out from his parka when the icy wind and haze permitted.

"Rick," he heard Clare's voice inside his own head clear as if she were standing alongside him, "you're getting too old for this kind of thing." Clare was his daughter. Somehow, amazingly, the years had spilled along and now she was a thirty-four-year-old woman, a journalist who was forever placing herself precisely in the center of the most dangerous places on earth. When she graduated from Columbia, she went freelance to Somalia, where civil war and armed insurrection were spilling blood by the tanker load. Since then, she'd been all over the Middle East and Africa as a correspondent with several papers. Now she was in Iraq with the *Times*. Clare was always in Rick's thoughts, and because the voice in his head had sounded so real, he answered her out loud. He said, "You're right, sweetheart. I'm getting old." As he spoke he looked up the beach and again saw the diminutive wavering human figure in the white coat, only now it appeared to be partly in the water, immersed to the waist—except that the figure was steady, solid in the roiling water, as if it were standing in a backyard pool, impossible in a turbulent ocean in the midst of a storm, and then, as he watched openmouthed, the wind blew back a hood of some kind, and long black hair whipped out and flew around wildly before a wave came in and washed the figure away, leaving only violent water and the mirroring images of clouds and ocean.

Rick took one quick step forward, as if, for a heartbeat, he would rush to the aid of someone who had just been pulled under the water, but he knew with certainty what he had just seen had to be an illusion—a human being doesn't stand upright and motionless in turbulent water—and so he stopped and tried to unravel the possibilities while the wind and snow buffeted him, and then he turned around, still trying to figure out what he had seen, and let wind push him back against the dunes and forward to the parking lot. White driftwood blown along the beach by high winds was the best explanation he could come up with—and that was extraordinarily hard to believe. Through the snow and mist, in the dim storm light, it was conceivable that a piece of driftwood might look like a human figure—but what explained the hood blown back and the black hair blowing in the wind? Still, by the time he reached his Jeep, he had pushed the vision out of mind. It was an illusion of some sort, a trick of mind and weather. What might have amazed him as a young man merely interested him now, if that. He had seen something odd and at least a little bit mystifying. Okay. Fine.

When he got back to his house, he found Clare waiting for him, Clare who was supposed to be sweltering somewhere in the desert heat of Iraq. The storm had just started a few hours earlier, and there were already three or four inches of snow on the ground. He had gunned the engine to climb the steep part of his driveway, and when he parked where the blacktop leveled out, the front bumper of the Jeep up against the house, he found himself looking into the big bay window a few feet in front of him, where Clare was sitting on the window shelf looking out, just as she did when she was a child. Even through the blowing snow, he could see a look of grief on her face, and he guessed she was dismayed that he had been out driving around somewhere while the media were screaming for people to stay in their homes and off the roads—this was the storm of the century approaching, the storm of the millennium, etc. He smiled a big toothy smile, both to signal that everything was fine and at the joy of seeing her there safely at home—the pure pleasure of that affecting him like a drug, a sense of relief washing through him, his worry over her a constant pressure he wasn't even aware of until it relaxed some, as it did now seeing her.

Out of the car, in a little pocket of stillness as the wind dropped away for a moment, he stepped up to the window and pressed his nose against an icy pane of glass, trying to get a laugh out of his solemn-looking daughter. She was small, five-five, and petite, like her mother. At thirty-four, in her brown leather boots, crisp blue denims, and pretty green blouse, she might easily be mistaken for a college girl. She pulled her knees to her chin and raised her eyebrows, making a face that said *Well, aren't you coming in?* He moved back from the window, but couldn't pull himself away from the pleasure of the moment, the surprise of seeing her safe in his home, beautiful and looking vibrantly healthy, if also tense and worried, which showed in the lines around her mouth and jaw and in the telltale way she fingered her hair, an old habit from her childhood, combing through layers of hair, playing at it thoughtlessly, something she did when anything was even a little bit wrong, like, perhaps, worrying about her father out driving around in a storm. When she knocked on the window and opened her mouth, miming amazement at his failure to get in out of the weather, he started for the front door, and then hurried as a blast of wind whipped over the rooftop bringing down a thick curtain of snow.

Inside, as soon as he unzipped his coat, she met him with a hug around the neck that pulled her onto her toes. Rick, at a little over six feet, bent down to her embrace. He wrapped his arms around her waist, lifted her off the ground, and pulled her into the pillowy down of his parka. "What," he asked, as he kissed her on the top of her head, "are you doing here?"

"My God!" she said. "You're freezing!" She kissed him on the forehead before pushing away from him and wrapping her arms around her chest. "You're an ice cube," she said. "Look at you! There's ice—" She reached up to touch his eyebrows and his beard, then tugged at the zipper of his parka. "You need to get into warm clothes." She moved back from him, put her hands on her hips, and looked him over. Her eyes filled with tears, which she quickly wiped away. "I'll make you some tea," she whispered. "Go get yourself out of those clothes." She turned her back to him and went into the kitchen.

Rick pulled off his boots and tossed them in a corner, under the hall tree, where he hung up his coat next to Clare's, which was a long, bright white quilted parka—much like the one he had seen on the beach. When the connection registered, he was filled with a sense of dread at the eeriness of it, at the plain spookiness of it—but he quickly pushed that strangeness out of mind and made himself return to the current, very real, situation. Clare wasn't a crier. Their reunions were usually full of joshing and hugs and long talks. Not tears. She wasn't an emotional person, which was something, he guessed, she had learned from him. Rick's response to emotional situations was to fall into a trance of detachment and objectivity, as if every cell in his body were purely and simply interested in discerning the best course of action. It was just the way he was. Paige, his wife, Clare's mother, had been killed in Jordan. They were living in Amman—this was 1972—during the violence after Munich. An Al-Fatah bomb went off inside the house of an Arab National Union official when Paige happened to be walking past outside. A piece of shrapnel killed her. She was the only fatality. He remembered that day and those weeks with preternatural clarity. He was Clare's age. Clare was eleven weeks old. He had made all the necessary arrangements with detachment and calm. A month after Paige's murder, he was back in the States with Clare. He quit his job with the World Bank so he could be a full-time father, and he had been living ever since off investments and consulting work. Essentially, at age thirty-four, he had retired.

"Rick . . ." Clare peeked into the hallway. She'd been calling him by his first name since she turned twelve, though occasionally she slipped and called him Dad. "I'm okay," she said. "Quit standing there like a statue trying to think of what to do, and go get out of those clothes and into something dry and warm." She offered him a quick, reassuring smile and then disappeared again into the kitchen.

Rick followed her. She was standing at the stove, her hands clasped around the handle of the oven door, staring at a thin line of steam escaping from the spout of a red kettle. "Clare," he said, "what is it?" Then he added, stupidly, "Is something wrong?" Because something obviously was wrong. There were tears in her eyes again as she watched the kettle begin to steam.

She wiped a hand across her face and shook her head as if she were about to say, *No, there's nothing wrong really*, but instead she said, "Yes. There is something wrong," and then laughed at herself. She turned away from the stove and tea kettle and said, again, "I'm okay," and pointed up the short flight of stairs to the bathroom. "Get . . . de-iced," she said. "I can't talk to a snowman!"

Rick touched the ice in his beard with some surprise, having already quit thinking about the storm outside.

"We'll talk over tea." Clare wiped her eyes again and said, referring to the tears, "Part of this is— I've been through something, and I'm, just, really happy to be home."

Rick cocked his head, waiting for more, but Clare again

pointed up the stairs and then turned back to the tea kettle as it started to whistle.

Rick touched her shoulder and hesitated another second before, reluctantly, heading upstairs.

In the bathroom, he quickly stripped off his parka and the ski pants and bib under it, and tossed them into the bathtub. From the rack, he grabbed a towel to dry his face and hair. As he looked in the mirror, he pushed longish gray hair back from his face, neatening it with his fingers and the palms of his hands, and it occurred to him he grew more bearlike with every passing day. His once athletic body had grown bulky as his waistline expanded. He had been living alone too long, he thought, with no one to bother him about his appearance. He needed badly to lose some weight. He ran his fingers through his hair one last time and padded down to the kitchen in heavy wool socks.

Clare was sitting at the table, holding her teacup in both hands, gazing up at him. She looked pretty with her straight brown hair cascading over the muted green of her blouse. A cup of tea awaited him across the table from her. "How did you get here?" he asked. He pulled out his chair and settled into the seat.

"Someone dropped me off."

"Who? In this weather?"

"I don't know him, really," she said, the tears gone, her voice placid. "He's new in the office. He insisted."

Rick sat back in his chair, as if he needed greater distance to absorb this information. "He insists on driving you out to Long Island in the middle of a winter hurricane, and you don't know him? What? Does he have a thing for you?"

"Not like that," Clare said. "Look," she made a face that dismissed the issue. "Guy gave me a ride. It's not a big deal."

"Okay," Rick said. "So? Why are you home? What have you been through? What, honey, is going on?"

Clare exhaled dramatically. "Listen," she said, her eyes fixed on her teacup, "there's so much . . . First—" She looked up at Rick. "I got back a few days ago. I didn't call because I wanted to work some things out before we talked."

"Have you been . . . hurt?" he asked. "Has something—"

"I haven't been hurt," she said. "I was threatened. I was almost— My life was threatened."

"Are they taking you out of Iraq?"

"Yes, but it's more complicated. I might get cut loose altogether," she said, "because of what happened."

"They're going to let you go because your life was threatened?"

"Please. Dad . . ." She placed her hands flat on the table. "Let me explain all this. First, I'm here waiting for a call. They're going to let me go, or they're going to reassign me—someplace in the Middle East. Not Iraq. I'm done in Iraq."

Rick nodded, working hard not to show his pleasure at this piece of news.

"This is my career," she went on. "If they let me go . . . I don't know what's next." She was quiet for a moment then, as if trying to figure out how to go on. Rick had to struggle to keep himself from reassuring her, from telling her everything would be okay, just tell him, just tell Dad what happened—as if she were still a child and he had the power to fix all her problems, which, he knew, had never been the case.

"All right," she said. "This is going to be hard for me to tell you, which is another part of the reason I waited to come out here. So, please, Dad, just listen."

"I promise," he said. "I'll just listen. I also promise I won't judge." Clare's face tightened in anger at that, and he watched a complex mix of emotions distort her expression in a way that made her ugly for a moment. He took a sip of his tea.

"First—" she said. "You have to understand— To get one single bit of reliable information anywhere in Iraq— Forget our side. Truth is, absolutely, the first casualty." She looked away for a moment, as if trying to gather her thoughts. "I'm trying," she said, "to report on the insurgency. This is, from the start, tricky. You're dealing with people who are killing American soldiers, who are killing Iraqis. They're in the business of killing. It's so, difficult, morally, every way— But my job is to report the story, to report it, and I can't— I'm not going to be a propagandist for the U.S. Army. I need to see for myself, to report what's going on, and you can't do that from one side's perspective only."

Rick gave Clare a look that said he wasn't an idiot. He didn't need this explained to him.

"All right," she said. "I made a contact inside a group of jihadis. This is near impossible for someone like me to do. It happened," she rapped the table with her knuckles, as if urging him to pay particular attention, "after I met an Arab woman named Sabiha. She represented herself as a freelancer. She had bylines from Al Jazeera to the *Monitor*. They all checked out. She moved into the hotel room next to mine, and we met in the hall one evening. We had drinks, we got friendly. Through her I made the contact with Othman. You would never— He was actually working in the fucking hotel."

Rick laughed uncomfortably. He had never heard Clare curse before. It was like being given a quick glance into her other life, the life where she had drinks in hotel bars and made contacts with killers.

"I'm telling you things you shouldn't know, Dad. I'm assuming you understand that."

Rick shrugged off the warning.

"All of Sabiha's stories fairly dripped with bias against anything in any way Western. She was more an Arab propagandist than she was a reporter. I wrote her off as a journalist. She practically gloated every time an American got killed. She'd be chirping, *Five Americans killed this morning!* Like I was supposed to join her for a drink in celebration, and I'm— I understood she was the best shot I had at making a contact somewhere—given she seemed to have contacts everywhere. It was like she worked for the insurgents. I wouldn't, at any time, have been surprised to find out she really did work for them." She leaned back in her chair. "I thought I was playing her, working her for the contacts. Only she was playing me from the start." She grimaced, as if disgusted with herself. "She takes the room next to mine, we conveniently meet— Perfect. She knew how I'd read her. She knew what I'd want from her. And she used me . . . like I was a novice."

"*Used* you?"

"She was one of ours." Clare got up, took both teacups from the table and stuck them in the microwave. "You pick the initials," she said. "We've got operations going on there that you never heard of and you never will hear of." She pressed a series of buttons and then slammed the microwave door hard enough to rattle the counter. When she turned to face Rick again, her face had reddened.

Rick said, "Clare, tell me what happened."

Clare took a deep breath and pushed on. "She was about to up the level of surveillance on these people," she said, "and she knew that would be risky. So what better than to introduce me to them right before she does it? This way, if they find out, they're not going to think of her—a sister, a sympathizer, she's practically writing press releases for them. They'll think of me. The American they didn't want to meet from the start. They only did it because of her influence, her pressure. She convinced them they needed an American reporter to tell their side. She promised them I could be trusted. She gave them a goddamned course in American journalistic ethics—and they went along, because of her, only because of her—and only reluctantly."

"And then that's what happened?" Rick said. "They figured out this surveillance thing . . . and they threatened your life?"

The microwave beeped loudly and Clare spoke through the beeping as if she didn't hear it at all. "They were going to kill me, Dad. I was going to be one of those tapes that wind up on the Internet." She looked down and her eyes were full of tears. "They were going to saw my goddamned head off," she said, "and I kept thinking— I kept imagining you watching the videotape—" She pulled her arm roughly across her eyes.

Rick felt that familiar focusing of attention that seemed, at times like this, to replace emotion in him. "Was this an actual, physical— Did they have you? Did they capture you?"

"They grabbed me off the street. Car pulled up, two seconds later I was on the floor in the back with an army-issued hood over my head. I never made a sound, it happened so fast. I didn't scream. Nothing. I just . . . waited."

"Did they hurt you?"

"Kicked me," she said, as if the detail were inconsequential. "Screamed at me."

"How did you— My God, Clare . . ."

"People like Sabiha— Like us over there," she squinted and backed away slightly, as if she were too disgusted to finish her thought. "Othman figured it out in two minutes," she said. "There were questions I couldn't answer, things I obviously didn't know. All I could have possibly done was go to the CPA and say, *Hey, I know this jihadi*—and that would not explain the net that all of sudden fell on them. It had to be Sabiha. We both knew it. There was this point where— They had me duct-taped to a chair, I'm answering questions, and then, it was like we both figured it out at the same moment. It was Sabiha. It had to be Sabiha."

"They let you go? When they figured that out?"

Clare was silent then. Her body seemed to grow heavier with the weight of what she was thinking. She met Rick's eyes and blinked and then said, softly, matter-of-factly, "They let me go because I gave her up. I gave them Sabiha."

"I don't get that," Rick said, quickly. "What do you mean, *you gave her up?* You said they knew. You said he'd figured it out himself."

Clare rubbed at a spot on the table with the heel of her hand. She was thinking, but it looked like she was trying to erase something. She said, "Just listen, Dad." She folded her hands together, interlocking fingers, as if in an effort to keep them still. "They would have killed us both," she said, "or held us both as hostages. They would not have let me go." She paused again, her gaze fixed on Rick. "Sabiha didn't go back to her hotel room that evening. She was, in fact, nowhere to be found. Which is part of what clued in Othman. Why would she disappear like that? And why wouldn't I? Why would I be strolling around outside the Green Zone without even a bodyguard? If I had a clue what was going on? If I knew? You see? I mean . . . Did she think he would miss that? Did she think he wouldn't pick up on that? I knew where she would be," she said, flatly, "and I traded my life for hers."

Rick shook his head slightly, hardly aware of it, as if some silent part of him was unwilling to accept this piece of news. He opened his mouth to say something, but no words came out.

Clare said, "It gets worse."

As if wanting to put off however this story could get worse, he asked, "How did you know where she was?"

"For someone who thought she was very smart," Clare said, "she wasn't. She underestimated them, and she underestimated me. There was a Kurd family working with one of the local councils. I figured them as U.S. operatives. So did everyone. I saw her with the father. I followed them and saw her slip in the back door of their home. This was weeks earlier. I thought, then, she's just trying to get a story. I thought she was doing what journalists do, gathering sources. That she was being secretive was no big deal, not then anyway. It wasn't healthy for Iraqis to associate with foreigners, any foreigners. So, I just figured, then, a story. She's looking for a story, for sources. But duct-taped to that chair, I saw the chances were excellent that's where she'd be."

"And that— You told them and they—"

"This is where it gets worse." She opened the microwave as if the bell had just sounded. She put Rick's cup in front of him and took her seat at the table again. "I know it must be hard to listen to this," she said. "Bottom line, I gave up a fellow American. I understand that. But . . . I feel like . . . You're the only person on earth who might—"

"What?"

Clare looked down and didn't answer. The look of grief Rick had noticed when he first saw her intensified then, spread all through her, was visible in the way her shoulders slumped and her head hung over the table.

"All right," Rick said. He reached across the table to place his hand over hers.

She slid her hand away. "I had to take them to the house. I was worried because I knew they had children: two little girls and a infant. They assured me they only wanted Sabiha. That once they had her, they'd let me go, and no one else would be hurt. They told me this on their honor—which means something to them. I knew they'd do what they said. I didn't tell them," she added, tapping one finger on the table for emphasis, "until I had his word. They would take Sabiha and they would let me go. I had his word. *She* was the combatant," she said, as if making her argument to Rick. "*She* set all this in motion." Clare had to pause for a breath, the telling upsetting her. "I knew they'd let me go," she said, almost in a whisper. "What I didn't count on was that Sabiha might be prepared to resist such an exchange."

"Jesus," Rick said, knowing without having to be told what was coming. He held his head in his hands, covering his eyes.

"We went in two cars. Othman went in with four others. They left me in the car with a driver and another guy in the backseat, next to me. All I heard was the gunfire. It didn't last long. Othman came out alone, bleeding and limping. He pulled me out of the car, spat in my face, and left me there."

"The children?" Rick said, and when he looked up Clare was nodding. Her eyes were dry and her face was tight, hard.

"When I went in the house—" she said, and then apparently couldn't go on, though her expression remained unchanged.

"All of them?" Rick pressed, hoping for something, some small ray of light.

"All of them," she said, angrily, as if throwing the words in his face, as if to say, if you have to know, here it is. "The infant was shot in the face," she said.

"All right," Rick said, wanting her to stop. "All right."

They were both quiet for a long while as wind battered the house, banging into windows and pummeling doors. The dim light outside faded away, and the darkness of the spaces surrounding the kitchen grew more pronounced, until it felt to Rick like the brightly lit kitchen table, situated directly under a ceiling light, was at the center of a stage, and in the surrounding darkness an audience sat quietly watching them. After awhile, he got up and turned on more lights. He looked out the living room's glass doors and saw the wind had blown the snow in the yard up against the fence, where it was sculpting it in waves, like a mountain's hollows and rises. Though the wind was blowing hard, it was snowing only lightly. Not much more had accumulated since he had returned from the beach.

When he sat down again at the table, he picked up the conversation where they had left off. "So he lied to you," he said, "this Othman. He told you they would just take Sabiha, but then they executed the whole family."

Clare was staring at her teacup, holding it in both hands, looking a million miles away. She pulled herself out of her own thoughts and looked up at Rick as if surprised to find him there. "No," she said. "I don't think that's what happened. Othman—on his own terms—could be trusted. No," she repeated, as if confirming her own opinion to herself. "They went in; Sabiha, the Kurds, they defended themselves, probably before anything could even be said. And once the guns were out . . . Once the shooting started . . ."

"But the Kurd family—"

"They were working with Sabiha." Clare got up from the table. She sounded frustrated. "You're not getting this," she said. "The Kurds were ours. Sabiha was ours. They were all working for us. Once I understood that Sabiha was ours, the rest was obvious. That's how I knew where she'd be. Do you get that?" she asked, her words clipped and angry.

"Okay," Rick said. "I didn't fully—"

"There were enough weapons in that house—" she said, as if she hadn't even heard Rick try to explain himself. She got up and started toward the bedroom stairs, then turned around in the kitchen doorway. "All their guns were current U.S. issue," she said. "Not the ancient shit the Iraqis use. There was enough weaponry for a small army. Plus sophisticated communications in a back room."

"All right," Rick said, raising his voice to get her attention. "Still, you don't know what happened in that house. You don't know who's responsible—"

"I'm responsible," she said, as if there were no question.

"No—"

"Please, Rick," she said. "I'm not interested in equivocations. I knew what I was doing. I traded Sabiha's life for mine. It's basically that simple. And the rest . . . the children . . . I have to live with that. I'm responsible." She sat down on the stairs, more dropped than sat, as if all the strength suddenly went out of her. She pulled her hair back in a ponytail and held it with both hands. "Listen to me, Dad," she said. "No one knows any of this for certain. I've told them all I was kidnapped, held, and then brought to that house and kept in the car when Othman and the others went in. From the car, I heard gunfire. When Othman came out wounded and in a panic, I was able to escape. I jumped out of the backseat as the car screeched away." She made a horrible, pained sound that Rick saw was supposed to be a laugh. "It's that last part," she said, "that nobody's buying."

"You don't think," Rick said, "if you explained what happened fully—"

"To whom?" Clare raised her voice, as if shocked at the prospect of explaining herself to someone. "Rick, do you understand— If one of Sabiha's circle gets it in her head that I was sympathetic with the insurgents— If one of her good friends, let's say, someone who loved her, who went to Harvard or Yale with her—Yale Drama given the actor she was—if one of them gets it in her head I was working with that group, I can disappear. Or even if someone decides I should be punished—it's not hard to interpret what I did as treason—I wind up in some black hole in Romania as an enemy combatant, with no recourse to you or anyone. You can tear your hair out all you please. Do you understand? Do you understand the danger?"

Rick didn't say anything. He watched her sitting on the stairs, her eyes full of anger and fear. After a moment, he nodded.

"I think it's touch and go as it is," she said. "They figure— They're not dumb. They can figure out that I pretty much must have made some kind of deal to get out of that situation alive. But they don't *know*. The *Times* doesn't know. No one knows for sure. It could have happened the way I said. And as long as they don't know, I'll be all right. I think I'll be all right."

"Okay," Rick said. He wanted to touch her, to comfort her some way, because she was his daughter, to say something about the horrors of war, about the terrible things it makes people do— but he knew better. He heard himself whisper, "You don't want me to say anything, do you, Clare? You just need me to listen."

She looked down at her feet and then back up to Rick as if that wasn't quite it, as if there was something else she needed from him. She watched him for a long moment before speaking again. "I was thinking of you," she said. "You lost your wife to this. You shouldn't lose your daughter." She paused and added, "I kept imagining you watching a videotape of me getting killed. I kept imagining what that would do to you."

Rick watched Clare carefully as she sat there on the stairs. He felt something more was coming. She had let go of her hair, and her arms dangled loosely at her sides.

"Rick," she said, "Mom's murder killed most of you. You kind of died there with her, didn't you? You didn't really survive it. Not really."

"You don't survive such a thing," he said, without thinking. "Not really."

Clare watched him, and for an instant an expression very near contempt seemed to cross her face. Then she pulled herself to her feet and climbed the stairs to her old bedroom.

For more than an hour, Rick sat at the kitchen table in the hope Clare might come down for a drink of water or something to eat. In the quiet house, even the softest sounds she made in her bedroom drifted down the stairs, so that he felt like he was watching her as she sat on the edge of her mattress and opened her bedside window a crack to let in fresh air. He heard her rise and pace the floor. He heard her lie down and get up again. He heard the soft electronic sounds her cell phone made as she dialed numbers three times in the space of an hour or so, each time leaving a brief message on someone's machine, the message tone clear if the words weren't. Eventually, he got up and turned off the lights in the kitchen and the surrounding rooms so that he could stretch out on the couch, in the dark, and watch the wind through the glass doors of the living room as it blew snow in great blasts and flung it in mounds against the fence.

After a while, a plow went past the house, its revolving orange light flashing through the room accompanied by the rhythmically repeating warning tones of the vehicle and the rough scraping noise of the massive blade pushing along the street, throwing off the accumulated snow. He went to the front door to see how much snow the plow had piled up in his driveway and found a small hill of it there, maybe two feet high. It was still snowing, but lightly. In the night sky, thick bands of gray clouds tumbled and rolled, low and fast, pushed along by powerful bursts of wind. From behind a double-insulated glass door, Rick listened to an animal wind snarling and watched it twist and swirl, given shape and body by the haze of snow it carried and the artificial light from the street's lampposts, which rattled and vibrated in the storm.

When, eventually, he closed the door, he found himself facing the dark interior of his house. It was still relatively early in the evening, and he considered turning on the television to watch the news and weather. Instead, he made his way through the dark house to his den, where he turned on the desk lamp so he could look through the library of books lining the gleaming wooden bookcases built into the den's four walls. He thought he might start one of the several novels he had bought recently only to leave unopened on a shelf, but found himself gravitating toward his collection of books on the history and politics of the Middle East. His own experience there and Clare's work had fostered an abiding interest in the region. He pulled out a recent volume on the American occupation of Iraq, but as soon as he held the book in his hand he felt an overwhelming tiredness, as if the book somehow radiated all the endless heartache that had spewed out of that little corner of the world, back to the birth of Islam, the birth of Christianity, back to the ancient tribes of the Jews, and before, so that just the thought of opening it exhausted him. He put it back on the shelf and went down to the living room couch with a novel.

The light was still on in Clare's bedroom, a bright yellow sliver of it seeping out under her closed door. From where he was stretched out on the couch, he could see up the stairs and along the hallway all the way back to her room. He placed the novel on his chest as he rummaged through his memories: Clare as a baby asleep on his shoulder, Clare as a child in her favorite black floppy hat, Clare in college. . . . The fight they'd had when she came home on break with a tattoo of a red lynx peeking tentatively but ferociously out of a protective green forest that covered a significant portion of a shoulder blade. He'd been furious. She'd been defiant. He told her it looked like the kind of tattoo a sailor might get, drunk in a foreign port—and when her eyes lit up with pleasure at the comparison, he'd stomped away into the den and locked the door. On the couch, with the wind screeching at the window, he smiled at that, at locking the door as if she might try to break it down to get to him. He fell asleep with the novel still open on his chest, remembering a night when she was a baby, not long after Paige's death. She had a cold and couldn't sleep and he had walked her back and forth in her bedroom, rocking her as he paced, her head on his shoulder, patting her on the back and talking to her softly until her weight shifted in the subtle way it does with sleep.

When he opened his eyes again, there was a pillow under his head, he was covered with Clare's quilted down comforter, and the novel was gone. At about the same moment he registered the familiar bluish light filling the living room window and figured out it was early morning, Clare pushed in through the front door bundled up and carrying a snow shovel. She was followed by an icy blast of air that bulled its way into the house. She smiled shyly at him and said, "Good morning. I tried not to wake you." She stomped her feet, kicking off snow, and went about taking off her gloves and coat.

"What are you doing up so early?" He wrapped the quilt around himself and shuffled to the window, where he saw she had already shoveled out the driveway. In the road, a pair of telephone lines were down, the raw blond wood spiked savagely where the poles snapped, high, near the transformers. A repair crew was already out there working. "Do we have power?" he asked.

"Not yet. You want some orange juice?" Clare shook off the cold and started for the kitchen. She had on boots and jeans and a black turtleneck sweater that made her fair skin look pale and not particularly healthy. "Phone guys said it'd be a couple of hours still."

Rick followed her into the kitchen holding the quilt wrapped around his shoulders, the length of it dragging behind him like a bridal train. "What's— Why are you up so early?" he asked again, as if it were the only question he could manage.

Clare stood in front of the refrigerator holding a glass of orange juice. She looked like she was thinking about her response.

"You already shoveled the driveway?" he said. "How long have you been up?"

"Didn't go to sleep." She took a sip of juice. "I was out there at around three-thirty, and—" She pulled her cell phone out of the pocket of her jeans and looked at the face of it. "It's a little after seven now."

Rick reached out from under the quilt to rub his eyes. He couldn't quite grasp what was going on. "Why," he asked, "would you shovel the driveway by yourself in the middle of the night?"

"Because someone will be here in a few minutes," she said, and the way she said it made it clear she understood that this would not make Rick happy and she was sorry about that. She added, as if to be sure he understood, "I'll be leaving with him, soon as he gets here."

Rick looked out the kitchen window into the backyard, as if to be sure he hadn't dreamed the whole snowstorm. "In this weather? Where are you going? Are the roads even passable?" He sat down at the kitchen table. "Clare . . ."

"Storm of the century dumped about a foot and a half of snow before it moved out to sea." She rinsed her glass out in the sink. "The major arteries are all clear. Some of the back roads are still a mess, but the guy drives a Land Rover, so— Roads shouldn't be a problem."

"But why?" he asked, his voice shooting up a little, so that he sounded almost like a teenager. "Why do you have to go?"

Before Clare could answer, her cell phone rang. She flipped it open, listened a second, and then went to the living room window. "You're two houses away," she said into the phone. "We're the driveway with the red Jeep, on your left. I'll be right out."

Rick said, "He's not even going to come in? Why not? Who is this guy, Clare?"

"Just a guy," she said, and she snapped her phone closed.

Rick took her by the arms and held her in front of him. "You can't just leave with some guy and I have no idea—"

"All right, listen." She stepped back out of his grasp. "He's someone's been assigned to protect me from threats—"

"What threats?"

"Let me finish. I don't know what threats either. He won't— He says he can't get into particulars."

"Well who is he?" Rick asked, his voice shooting up again. "Do you know for sure who he is?"

"He's Homeland Security," Clare said, as if running out of patience, "and I have to go."

"Do you believe him? That he's protecting you—"

"No," she said. "Please. He's here to make sure I don't go anywhere before they all decide what to do about me."

"Before who all decides?"

"I can't—" Clare pushed past him and started up the stairs to her bedroom. "I'm sorry, Dad," she called back. "I really— I have to go."

Rick dropped the quilt and followed her. With the power out, the house was dark and chilly as a cave. "Is there something else going on that I don't know about, Clare?" He asked his question alone in the shadowy hall, Clare having already disappeared into her room. "Is there something you're not telling me?" When he reached her room, he met her in the doorway, a red backpack flung over one shoulder as she pulled a black suitcase behind her. "Is there?" he asked again.

"I have to go," she said, looking through him. She pushed past him, out into the hall.

Rick took her by the arm. "You can't just walk off and leave me without any idea what's going on. It's not—"

"All right," she said, cutting him off by putting her hand flat against his chest.

Rick let go of her arm and put his hands up. His heart was beating fast enough to worry him slightly. "I'm sorry," he said. "But this—"

"Okay," she said, and she watched him for a moment.

Rick thought, again, he saw something close to contempt in her eyes. "Have I done something?" he asked.

"Look, Dad," she said. "I don't know what's happening for sure. All I know is, I have to go."

"At least tell me where you're going then. Are you going back to work? What happened with the *Times?* Did they call?"

"I called them," she said. "I asked for an indefinite leave, which they were more than happy to grant."

"What does that mean?" Rick asked, and after thinking another second, added, "But, why? I thought you wanted—"

"No," she said, as if the issue were decided. "I did want to go back. I thought I could put it all out of mind, put it all behind me. That I didn't have to—" She stopped and shook her head, as if she didn't want to say what she was thinking.

"Are you going to tell them what happened?" Rick said. "You said you couldn't do that. You said that was impossible."

"I don't know what I'm going to do." She looked down the hall toward the living room, and at the same moment, her phone rang again. She told the voice on the other end she was on her way out the door, and then she touched Rick's arm gently after putting the phone back in her pocket. "I have to go," she said, and pulled her suitcase behind her down the stairs and to the front door, where she stopped to put on her winter gear.

"You can work in the States," Rick said. "You can work for another paper."

"Not really." Clare reached down below her knees and pulled

up the long zipper to her coat. "Wherever I go, there'll be whispers." She slung her backpack over her shoulder again. "I don't think it's going to work, lying about it." She closed her eyes, as if to give herself a much needed moment of stillness. "I think I may just have to deal with it."

Rick grabbed her suitcase as she reached for it. "What does that mean, *deal with it?*" he said. "You said you couldn't tell them. You said it would put you in too much danger."

Clare opened the door, but before she stepped out, she said, "I don't want to run away. I don't think I can live like that." Suddenly, she seemed angry again. "This whole situation is miserable. I need to think it through. But I can't—" She stopped and took a breath and shook off the anger. "I can't run away. I don't think, for me— I don't think that will work."

Outside, when Rick hesitated in the doorway, she said, "You have my cell number," and then she held his head in her hands and kissed him hard on the forehead, before taking her suitcase from him and making her way carefully to a black Land Rover waiting in the mouth of the driveway.

Past the Land Rover, farther up the street, two more poles were down. When Rick took a few steps out into the cold so he could see in the opposite direction, past the row of hedges that lined his yard, he discovered several more poles snapped, their wires and wood and transformers littering the snow-covered blacktop along with garbage cans, a patio table, roof tiles, and various pieces of debris. He took one quick step toward the driveway, thinking he had to stop Clare from trying to drive through that mess, but he stopped just as quickly as he had lurched forward. He pushed his hands into the pockets of his coat and hunched his shoulders against the wind. In the driveway, Clare had just thrown her suitcase into the back of the Rover, and she was moving toward the passenger door as she looked up the street. When she stopped a moment to survey the damage, she pulled up her hood, and no sooner had she pulled it up than the wind blew it off again and her long hair whipped around her head—and the vision from the beach came back to Rick. He saw Clare duck and disappear into the car as if she were standing in turbulent water being pulled under by a wave. Before he could think of anything to do, she was slowly driving away, the black car winding along the street—but it felt like she was being pulled out to sea.

For a long moment he stood out in the weather as if stunned, and when a blast of wind charged him like a beast, with such ferocity it nearly knocked him down, he noticed a silvery flash of metal against the snow on the driveway—and he knew immediately it was Clare's cell phone. He hurried down to it, for a confused second thinking he could call her on it, could tell her to come back, she had dropped her phone, and when he realized the absurdity of that, he pressed the phone against his heart, as if it were a token of someone who was lost to him. For a long time he stood there staring out at the road, seeing again and again, first the image of a woman being swept away by a storm wave, and then Clare driving off in that black car.

Wind gusted and swirled along the street as he waited silently in the snow, holding the cell phone to his heart.

Mythmakers

On the ferry to Culebra, as we pulled into the dock, my father caught sight of a beautiful woman fixing lunch for a skinny boy in what looked like the town square, a small, polished stone area with a single tree and a few tables overlooking the Caribbean. The weather was gorgeous: sunlight on blue water lapping white coral beaches, on green hills rising over the sea, on the village's dizzying hodgepodge of brightly colored buildings. The woman in the square looked too young to be the mother of the scrawny boy she had just handed a sandwich. My father focused his binoculars on her just as she poured the boy a drink out of a thermos. The kid swallowed his drink in one long gulp and then walked off toward the water with his hands thrust deep in his pockets. She put the thermos down and looked out over the water.

This was my first vacation with my father in more than twenty years, since I was a boy myself, maybe eight or nine years old. I walked up beside the bench where he was sitting with his elbows on the table in front of him, peering through the binoculars. "Check out this woman," he said, when I sat down across from him. He tried to hand me the glasses.

"The one at the table in the square," I said, declining the binoculars. "I can see her."

"No," he said, insisting. "You have to check her out."

To placate him, I looked at her through the binoculars. She had dark hair and darker eyes and deeply tanned skin that fairly glowed in contrast with a yellow summer dress. "She's beautiful," I said, handing him the glasses back.

"And alone," he added, focusing on her again.

There was still a good bit of blue water sparkling between us and the dock, but the ferry was closing the gap rapidly. "What do you mean, she's alone?" I said. "She's got a kid. He's playing by the water."

He put the binoculars down on the table. "I mean she's by herself. If it's her kid, she's raising him alone."

"How can you possibly know that?" I heard the pitch of my voice rise, and I could tell I sounded angry—though I didn't mean to.

He gave me one of his amused-surprise expressions. He was in his mid-fifties, but he didn't look a hell of lot older than me. We had already been mistaken for brothers several times in the couple of days we'd been traveling. "Hey," he said. "Did you bring your meds?"

"Don't start," I said. "I'm just curious. What makes you say she's alone when she's got a kid with her?"

He smiled, and his eyes sparkled—which they did easily, and to the delight of many, especially women. His eyes were always a striking blue, but now they were emphasized by the steely gray of his hair, which he wore cut short, giving him a rugged, outdoorsman look. "I know," he said. "I can tell just by looking at her."

I didn't know whether I was amused or annoyed. "You're a character," I said. It came out sounding annoyed.

"Jeez . . ." He riffled through my shirt pocket, pretending to be looking for something. "Where's your Prozac?"

"Cut it out." I smiled despite myself, and pushed his hand away. "I'll bet you," I said. "A woman that good-looking is here with someone. I'll bet she's married, or traveling with someone."

"What do you want to bet?"

"Tonight's dinner. Best restaurant we can find on the island."

"All right," he said. "Deal." He stood up and ruffled my hair as if I were still ten years old, and then walked off toward the stern of the ferry where people were lining up to disembark.

On the dock, crowds of Puerto Ricans headed straight for taxis to the beach. I headed for the square, leaving my father to call for a ride to the villa. The atmosphere on the dock was festive, as if there wasn't a single pressured, anxious soul in the entire throng of people. Beyond the line of taxis, the crowd thinned, and I stepped into scorching sunlight to find the woman in the yellow dress watching me unabashedly. Our eyes met, I smiled, she smiled back, and I approached her table. I thought I would initiate a conversation by asking directions to our villa, but she spoke first. "Do I look the same to the naked eye," she asked, "as I do through binoculars?"

I blushed, unable to think of a quick response. While I was thinking, I slipped off my backpack and dropped it on the stone bench that followed the contour of the table. Then I looked at her, as if studying her. I said, "You seem more animated in person than you do from a distance."

"Animated," she repeated. "That's new. *Animated.*" She nodded approvingly.

"Thank you," I said. Before I could think of anything else to add, she looked over my shoulder. I turned around to find my father approaching. His eyes were fastened to hers, and when I turned back to her, the expression of approval had melted into something different, into precisely the same expression I had just seen on my father's face: it was a look of recognition, as if they knew each other, and for a moment I was convinced that was the case, that they were going to turn out to have known each other from home. It wouldn't have been impossible. She looked to be a little older than me, though still much younger than my father, which was just about the age of the long line of women he had been dating since his last divorce.

Her expression changed again by the time my father reached the table into one suddenly polite and friendly—and much less playful. "Kelly," she said, extending her hand to me.

"Ron," I said, shaking her hand. "And this is my *father*—"

"Henry," Dad said, and shook her hand cordially.

"—before you flatter him by asking if we're brothers."

"Of course he's your father," she said. "You can see it in his eyes."

Dad sat across from Kelly. "Did Ron say why he accosted you?"

"I accosted him."

"You did?"

"Yes, of course. Do you think it's every day such handsome men arrive in tiny Culebra?"

"Yes," Dad said. "Certainly."

"Well," Kelly said. "Almost every day. Why are you two in Culebra? How long are you staying?"

"Just one night. Ron's treating me to a week of island-hopping."

Kelly looked my way, and I had the feeling for a brief moment she might have forgotten I was there.

"We're bonding," I said. "I'm looking at thirty in a couple of months. I thought it was time to try to bond with the old man before he up and dies on me, or develops Alzheimer's or something."

Kelly gave me a slight smile and turned back again to meet my father's eyes. "You guys look pretty bonded to me," she said.

Dad and I looked at each other and said, at exactly the same moment, "Not really," which made all three of us laugh.

"Maybe more than we think," my father said.

She said, "Did you say how long you were staying?"

"Just one night," I answered, trying to wrestle her attention back in my direction.

"And," my father added, "it turns out that it's up to you which one of us pays for dinner tonight."

"Me?"

"He made a bet with me," I said. "That you were unattached."

"Oh . . . well." She turned to Henry. "You lose."

"Too bad," he said. "I really didn't want to be wrong."

"Thank you," she said. "I'm flattered. But you must have seen my son, didn't you?"

I gestured toward the water, where her son was talking to another boy, his white skin glaring in contrast with the other boy's dark skin. "That's him, isn't it?" I said. "Cute kid."

"He's not your everyday child," she said. "If you get a chance to talk with him, you'll see."

We all turned to look again at her son as a battered red Yugo pulled up to the square. The driver honked twice, cheerfully.

Kelly said, "There's your ride. Listen," she added, hurriedly. "You're only staying the day, you have to come out with us this afternoon. My husband has the best dive boat on the island, and you can't visit Culebra and not see the reefs. It's impossible. So," she said. "I'll make the reservations for you?"

I looked at my father. He looked at me. "Sure," he said.

"Sounds good to me," I added.

"It's done then. I'll see you both at twelve thirty sharp on the dock."

As we approached the driver of the Yugo, I asked my father, "What's the plan? Do you want to ask where we find the most expensive restaurant on the island, or should I?"

It turned out Kelly was a little older than I had guessed. I found out her exact age within a few minutes of arriving on the dock with my father, where we met Jake and Steven and a dozen tourists going out for an afternoon of snorkeling. Jake was Kelly's husband. He was a big guy with a beer gut and an easygoing manner. Kelly introduced us to him, he shook our hands, and then he went about stowing everyone's gear on board his boat, which looked to be about forty feet of glistening white paint and chrome. Steven was the scrawny boy from the square, Kelly's son, only he was cleaned up and dressed nicely now in blue shorts and a red T-shirt, with a new Baltimore Orioles cap pulled down low on his forehead. Even with the baseball cap, the kid looked too serious. After Kelly introduced us all, she took my father by the hand, led him on board, and started showing him around the boat. I watched them walk away. Kelly was wearing white shorts, just snug enough to stop a man's heart. My father had bought a safari hat, which was dangling now between his shoulder blades, held by leather cords around his neck. It lent a roguish look.

Steven turned to me and said, "She's thirty-five, you know. I'm going to be twelve soon, even though I know I look really young for my age. Everyone always thinks she's like my older sister or something, but she's really thirty-five years old." He said thirty-five as if it denoted unbelievable old age.

I said, "I'm going to be thirty myself in a few months."

He looked at me as if to say "Yeah? So?" A moment later, he thrust his hands in his pockets, looked down at his shoes, and then got on board without another word.

By the time we pulled away from the dock, all the passengers were clustered in the back of the boat exchanging personal information: who worked where, who did what, where everyone was from. Kelly leaned against the railing alongside my father, and I drifted toward the bow, where I watched the land slide away as we headed out into an open expanse of water that was robin's egg blue far as I could see. After a while my thoughts started gravitating toward the project I was heading up at work, and the woman I was currently dating. Neither meant much to me. When thinking about them started to make me feel surly, I headed back for the stern and the company of other passengers. On the way, I passed a door that led down several steps to a lower deck. I followed the steps to a cabin, where I found Steven sitting on a cot under a porthole, reading a book. He had an assortment of pillows scattered behind him like a throne.

He didn't look surprised to see me. Neither did he look particularly happy. "Hey," I said. "What are you reading?" I sat down on the bottom step.

He put the book on the cot beside him and folded his hands in his lap. "*Masks of God*," he said, softly. He looked me up and down, and I imagined what he saw: a man, dressed conservatively in khaki slacks and a white knit shirt, with brown eyes and slightly pale skin from a job that kept him indoors all day in front of a computer. While he was looking me over, I wished I had bought a hat like my father's. He had bought it in a shop on the way to the boat, and I had considered buying one too, but I knew it wouldn't look right on me. Besides, I would have felt absurd wearing the same hat as my father.

I'd never heard of the book the kid was reading. I asked, "What's it about?"

He touched the fat white paperback by his thigh. "This section," he said, "is about gods and heroes of the European West."

"Gods and heroes? Is that what you read now in— What grade are you in?"

"I'm in a distance-learning program for gifted students." He sounded proud of himself.

"No kidding," I said. "Your mom—"

"She's not my mother," he said. "She was my mother's best friend."

I waited for him to continue. Apparently, though, he had no intention of continuing. He stared at me. I said, "What happened to your mother?"

He placed the palm of his hand flat on the paperback, as if it were a Bible and he were about to take an oath. "She died in a diving accident. She went into a cave and got caught in currents that dragged her through coral. It tore up her diving gear. She drowned." After several long seconds of my sitting there looking at him, at a loss for anything to say, he continued. "Why?" he said. "Did she tell you she was my mother?"

I nodded. "She referred to you as her son."

"She does that with strangers," he said. "It's easier than explaining."

"Oh," I said. "I see. And Jake? Is he your father?"

"Uh huh," he said. "He's an alcoholic, though. He's always been. Even before Mom drowned. Sometimes I'm not even sure he really knows anything's changed."

"He's an alcoholic?"

"He's drinking right now. Want me to show you where he keeps the beer?"

"That's okay," I said.

"It wouldn't be so bad," he went on, "except it's like he doesn't really care about anything else."

"I'm sorry about that," I said. "That's sad." I looked away. I was suddenly very sorry that I had ventured below deck and initiated this conversation.

But the kid was rolling now. "You're grown up," he said. "And you still go on vacation with your father. I wish I had a father who'd take me on a vacation. I've never been any farther than Puerto Rico, and that was with my mom."

I said, "It's me taking him on vacation. And it's probably not like you're thinking. I really hardly know the man. He divorced my mother when I was ten, and I've only seen him occasionally since. He's my father, but I hardly know him. That's what this vacation is about. I'm trying to get to know him a little better."

"Why would you want to do that?" the kid asked. He leaned closer to me. "If he left you," he asked, "why would you want to get to know him better?"

"Because he didn't leave me," I said. "He left my mother."

"But you said he didn't stay in touch. You said you only saw him occasionally."

I laughed and said, "Well, yes, you've got a point."

"So why would you want to get to know him better?"

I looked up the stairs to the main deck. "It's hard to explain," I said. I crossed the cabin and sat beside him. I put my hand on his knee. I must have wanted to tell him something, but no words came as I sat there with my hand on his knee, looking him in the eyes.

The silence between us seemed like it might go on for days. Finally, he said, "So why'd he leave you? Was there a reason?"

"A woman," I said. "Half his age. Very pretty."

"Did you like her?"

"Never knew her. That was his second wife. He's just recently divorced his fourth. He trades them in every five years or so."

The kid was studying me again. "So," he said, sounding like he was about to sum things up. "Your father's a philanderer; mine's an alcoholic. My mother's dead. Yours?"

"Cancer."

"Great," he said, stone serious. "We should be best buddies." He got up and left the cabin, leaving me sitting on his cot. I picked up his paperback and looked at the cover, which pictured a creature half man and half beast. On deck, I heard women laughing. I guessed my father might have told one of his jokes. He could be a very funny guy when he wanted. Then I heard the engines groan, and felt the boat slow, and I figured it was time to go snorkeling.

I wasn't surprised when Kelly showed up at our villa that night. It was a little after nine, and my father and I were sipping martinis on the balcony, which had a gorgeous 180-degree view of the sea and the harbor. We had just come back from a mediocre dinner at a cheap restaurant. Our table was outside, though, on a dock—and that made up for the rest. I offered to share the cost, but Henry refused.

On the way back to the villa, we took a leisurely walk along the beach, which was almost spoiled when I had the bad taste to bring up my mother's death a few years earlier. He hadn't come to the funeral. He sent a card. At the time, I was furious with him, but I asked him about it not because I was angry or wanted an answer, but because I thought it might push the conversation, which had been mostly about seashells and brain coral, a little deeper, a little closer to something like intimacy. He didn't answer for a long time, and then he just shrugged and said, "That was such a long time ago."

"Just a couple of years," I said. "Not that long."

He massaged his temples hard, with his fingertips. "No," he said. "The whole relationship. With your mother." Then he was silent, looking off over the water.

It was a strange moment. It was as if he was trying to remember my mother.

I considered reminding him that he had been married to her for more than ten years, and that, after he left, she not only never remarried, she never so much as dated another man. That a week never went by when she didn't mention him once or twice. Then she was diagnosed with cancer, and that became her life for the next several years, until it eventually killed her. These thoughts, however, threatened to ruin the remainder of the evening. I pushed them away. The point of the vacation was to get to know my father, not to punish him or demand penance. Neither of which he would have allowed anyway, not without a battle. I turned the conversation back around to brain coral and driftwood, for which he seemed to be grateful.

Kelly arrived at the villa soon after we had settled into our deck chairs with drinks in hand. Henry got up to meet her at the door, which was down a short flight of stairs.

I said, "What about her husband?"

He said, "She says he's unconscious by nine every night."

"Oh. Sure," I said, with a slight laugh, though hell if I knew what I was laughing at. I asked, "Do you want me to leave?"

Before he disappeared down the stairs, he made a brief, ambiguous gesture with his head and hands, almost as if he was waving to me. It looked like he was dismissing my offer to leave—but he wasn't. He didn't. It was like the gesture pretended to dismiss my offer, didn't, and thus accepted it. It was ambiguous enough that I was still thinking about it when he led Kelly by the hand out onto the balcony.

"Do I get one of those?" she asked, smiling at me and gesturing toward my martini.

"Absolutely," I said. She was wearing black flats and a simple red dress with a squarish neckline cut to be revealing. Somehow, the dress and shoes together made her look as close to naked as a woman can look while fully dressed.

"I'll get it," my father said.

"No, no." I jumped up. "You like it dry?"

"Very."

"Take my seat," I said. "Sit."

"Are you sure?"

"Absolutely." I went about fixing her drink. "I was just about to take a walk along the beach before checking out your local cantinas."

"Oh," she said, twisting around in her seat. "Go to the Dinghy Dock. There's always a few women looking for a guy to talk to there."

"The Dinghy Dock," I said, handing her the martini, and then taking mine from the flat armrest of her chair. I still had a few sips left. "I enjoyed talking to Steven today," I said. "He's a remarkable kid."

"Isn't he?" she said. "Sometimes he's downright otherworldly."

Henry said, "I'm sorry I didn't get a chance to talk to him."

I asked, "Just how smart is he, anyway?"

"Off the scale," she said. "He came out of the womb reciting Shakespeare. When I took him home from the hospital he was already the most mature adult in the house."

My father and I both laughed at that.

"So," I said. "He *is* your son, then."

She nodded and appeared surprised by the question.

I finished my martini and put the glass down on the stairway railing. "I'll be back by eleven thirty," I said. "Enjoy your drinks."

Once outside, walking down a brick path lined with seashells, I wasn't unhappy things had worked out as they had. Henry and I didn't have a whole lot to say to each other anyway. I was beginning to suspect Henry didn't have a whole lot to say to anyone. The best kind of talking he did he was probably already beginning to do with Kelly. To myself, I said, aloud: "Things are the way they are."

From a plastic kiosk that covered a pair of garbage pails at the end of the path, a small voice replied, "What's that mean?"

I jumped, literally jumped, off the path and into the dangling branches of a tree with bright orange flowers.

"It's only me," Steven said, stepping out onto the road. "I didn't mean to scare you."

I held my hand over my heart and looked back toward the balcony of the villa.

"They can't see us from here," he said. "And I'm sure they're not listening."

I looked at him askance. "I'm not even going to ask what you're doing here."

"Why would you?" he said. When I didn't answer, he added: "All right if I walk back to town with you?"

I straightened out my shirt, brushing flower petals off my shoulder. "Sure," I said. "Why wouldn't it be?" I gestured toward the road like a gentleman stepping aside at a doorway.

For a little while, we walked in silence. Then Steven said, "Your father's a jerk, you know."

I didn't respond right away. I walked along a little farther, looking up at the stars, before I replied. I said, "Your mother seems to like him."

"I told you," he said. "She's not my mother. My mother's dead, like yours."

"Steven," I said. "Tell me something. Just how smart are you?"

He considered the question for a moment. "If you believe the tests," he said. "I'm a genius."

"Okay," I said. "Then. About my mother? She's not dead. I made that up. Out of sympathy for your story."

He turned quickly to look at me, surprised, and then turned back to look down at the road again just as quickly, as if embarrassed at having been caught off guard enough to be surprised. "Oh," he said. He sounded like he was taken aback and troubled by my news.

"Actually," I went on, "my mother's alive and well and happy. She's a remarkable woman. She was always something of an artist, but she didn't really discover her talent until she got divorced from my father. It's a long story, but . . . You'd like her. She's happy. She's beautiful. She's successful." I hesitated a moment, and added: "She's a very special woman."

Steven nodded, his eyes fixed on the pavement at his feet.

"And something else I lied about," I continued. "Henry? The guy with the safari hat on the boat? The guy Kelly's with in the villa right now?" I paused dramatically. "He's not my father. My father passed on long ago. I just don't like to tell people and get all into it. It's a complicated story."

For another minute, at least, Steven continued walking. He had no reaction. Then, for the first time since I'd laid eyes on him, I saw the kid smile. It started tentatively, as if he wasn't sure there was anything to smile about, and then he glanced over at me with a sidelong look, caught the expression on my face, and the smile blossomed, followed by a little laugh. "Go ahead," he said. "Tell me. I want to hear more."

"My story?" I said. "Okay. Sure. You have to give me a minute, though, to figure out how to tell it."

"No problem," he said, and he walked along beside me quietly, looking out to a web of stars. "Take your time," he added. He had a slight smile on his face, as did I. To anyone passing by, we would have looked like a father and son out for a walk on a pleasant Caribbean evening. We would have looked downright happy.

American Martyrs

Logan staggered down 34th Street toward The Strand and a morning walk along Manhattan Beach—or at least he felt like he was staggering. Anyone watching from one of the multimillion-dollar homes that lined both sides of the avenue would have seen a man who appeared to be in his forties—though he'd turned fifty a few months earlier—navigating a steep hill cautiously, taking his time, putting one foot in front of the other as the street dropped away with each step, spilling at a forty-five degree angle to a wide strip of beach and the ocean. Logan's head and eyes ached in a way that suggested sinuses, and he supposed some new, L.A.-bred pollutant or allergen might be the cause, though the mattress he was sleeping on in his sister's house could also be the problem. He'd taken some ibuprofen with his morning coffee, and he expected the throbbing in his head would abate shortly. Still, he felt as though he'd been thrown back several months and was staggering along some half-known street on one of his typical drunk return trips from nowhere to nowhere.

But Logan was sober. He was sober and it was six-thirty in the morning, and he was on his way to meet a sixteen-year-old girl under the Manhattan Beach pier.

He'd met Melody the night before at American Martyrs, a Catholic church that housed a local AA meeting. Becky, Logan's sister, had been driving him crazy with endless talk of what a miserable brute their father had been. He did know, didn't he, that Big Jack, which is what everyone in their hometown of Saltwell, Virginia, lovingly called their father, he did know that Big Jack had felt her up more than once when he was drunk out of his mind, didn't he? And did he have any idea what that did to a girl? And didn't he think her whole life had gotten so screwed up because of who else but that bastard, Big Jack? Logan wanted to ask, "Would that be the same Big Jack who used to come home blasted, with ice cream for you and a beating for me?" But didn't. He was a guest in her house for a week, which constituted the best vacation he could afford since retiring from the Saltwell police, and so he listened to her prattle until he was on the edge of taking his first drink in more than six months—and then he found the local AA meeting and went to it the following night.

Melody, the youngest of the dozen people seated on folding chairs arranged in a circle, had managed to get through the hour without saying a word beyond her name, first only, and her age, which she threw in as if announcing she was different from the rest of the much older crowd congregated in what looked like an elementary school classroom. Logan had noticed her first thing because how could anyone not notice her? He didn't know the names anymore for her manner of appearance—Goth, Punk, Skater, whatever, the names kept changing—but he tagged her at a glance as another screwed-up kid, not essentially unlike the screwed-up kids he had dealt with regularly as a cop, though she probably came from money, since her haircut and makeup alone looked like they cost more than some of the problem families in Saltwell brought home in a week. Still, underneath the straight-cut bangs and austere, flat, shoulder-length black hair, the raccooned mascara eyes, various dangling neck jewelry and a nose stud that looked like a small glowing-blue LED tacked into her lower right nostril and attached, apparently, to a string that hung out of her nose with a small button of some sort appended to it—despite all that, and despite the platform heels that added inches to her height and the black pantyhose decorated with circles of ghostlike faces and the slinky black dress that ended at midthigh, despite the body of a woman that her clothes barely covered, she still looked shockingly innocent. The baby-smooth skin of her arms and face had something to do with it, but mostly it was her eyes, which were wide and dark and reminded Logan of a little girl.

At the bottom of the 34th Street hill, Logan rubbed the bridge of his nose and his temples as he looked over the wide beach already busy with morning joggers and power walkers and people putting up volleyball nets, getting ready for the day's competition. Out on the ocean, surfers in black wet suits dotted the waves. Beyond the surfers a line of yellow kayaks was cutting through dark blue water, heading toward Palo Verde, and out past the kayakers, a pair of stand-up paddle surfers looked as though they were walking on water. Whenever Logan visited his sister, he left California with the impression that everyone on the West Coast was physically fit and in robust good health. Unconsciously, his hands slid down under the curve of his belly and he jiggled it, as if to gauge its weight and heft. He wasn't fat, but he wasn't in good shape either, certainly not compared to these joggers and volleyballers and surfers. Good enough shape though for a fifty-year-old alcoholic ex-cop from rural southwest Virginia. He looked at himself in the window-wall of somebody's beachside mansion and saw a tough-looking guy, a little taller than average, with short hair and skin already brown from a week in the sun. He appeared healthy enough, and in his leather sandals and chino shorts and black T-shirt, he thought he might even pass for a Californian, even with the slight—okay maybe a little more than slight—gut.

On the walk to the pier, Logan tried not to think about the past week with his sister. Becky was beautiful, had always been beautiful. Currently she was property rich and cash strapped. Twenty-two years ago, at the age of twenty-two, she'd married a man in his early sixties, the man who had owned the two-million-dollar-plus house where she was currently living while struggling to come up with the cash she needed for taxes and living expenses. When he died, the previous summer, at the age of eighty-five, he left her the house and a relatively small sum of money—a situation about which she was still furious. She'd been in court all year fighting with her late husband's three children over money. On top of that, she was now dating another man in his eighties, and she made not the slightest pretense about why. He was rich and she wanted his money. His children, however, were already interfering, trying to sour the relationship every opportunity they got, and hysterically threatening Becky with everything from legal action to a Mafia contract hit if their father married her. According to Becky, the marriage was already in the planning stages—though of course the children knew nothing about it. All week, Logan had to listen to an opera of suffering and complaint that alternated between Becky's current dramas and the great drama underlying all of her woes: her miserable father, Big Jack, who had left her, as she had told Logan a million times, incapable of a real relationship with a man.

Logan had nodded and grunted while Becky went on and on, and now, walking in bright sunlight between the mansions and the elaborate beachside gardens of The Strand, he had to work to keep her stories out of his head and allow himself to enjoy the sunlight and flowers and the occasional beautiful women who walked or jogged or bicycled past him. A veteran of three marriages, none of which had lasted more than two years, thanks to his drinking, he was himself between women. He broke up with his last girlfriend at exactly the four-month mark, which, for Logan, appeared to be some kind of magically predetermined relationship limit. With the exception of the three marriages, all of his relationships ended in approximately four months, and most of them followed the same pattern. First month he was wildly in love and he worked like hell to get the woman to reciprocate. When, somewhere in the second month she gave in and returned the sudden rush of love—that was the high point, and it lasted a few days to a few weeks before he started rapidly falling out of love. Usually things would drag on a few more months before ending badly. This last relationship had ended particularly badly—though it did have the unexpected and wonderful side effect of sending him to AA again, which in turn had led to six months and counting of sobriety.

Things had ended in a bar, with both him and the girlfriend drunk, when he had punched her in the face hard enough to loosen three of her front teeth—something he would be paying for, in multiple ways, for the next several years. Big Jack may have felt up Becky a few times, but he never beat her. She was his beautiful girl, and he never once picked her up by the hair and smashed her face into the plasterboard wall (that was Logan) or put her in the hospital for a week after beating her with her favorite rolling pin (that was his wife, their mom, Cicy). Logan and Cicy,

Jack beat on regularly—especially Cicy, who had died before she made it to forty. Technically, from an infection that went crazy, but as far as Logan was concerned, Jack had beat her to death. The moment after Logan's fist connected with his girlfriend's face, he was sober—and in the dark light of that bar, while a pair of his friends wrestled him to the ground, he swore he would never take another drink, and if he ever hit a woman again he'd blow his own brains out immediately after.

When he reached the pier, Logan pulled Melody's note out of the pocket of his shorts. The day was gorgeous. Another Manhattan Beach morning full of bright sunshine and golden sand and beautiful people playing in the ocean and on the beach. Logan took a seat on a convenient bench and unfolded the torn piece of loose-leaf paper on which Melody had drawn a cartoonish likeness of herself down the right side of the page. Though the body of the figure looked like something out of a sexy video game, a Lora Croft Tomb Raider kind of body, all cleavage and curves, the face was unmistakably Melody's, especially the eyes. On the left side of the page she wrote, "I couldn't get up the courage to talk to you here, but I feel like we share a lot and I really would like to talk. Can you meet me under the Manhattan Beach Pier at 7 A.M. tomorrow? I know you probably won't be there, but I will. I need some help. Please." The handwriting was neat and precise, and the sentences were coherent and grammatically correct—including commas and question marks. So, she was literate and he was willing to bet, from the way she carried herself and from something he saw in her eyes, smart.

At the meeting, he had shared twice, both times about Becky. He'd portrayed her as even more of a screaming maniac than she really was, but one of the purposes of an AA meeting is to provide a space where people can vent—and he'd vented. He'd gone on for a while about the man Becky was currently dating—whom he'd had a meal with twice in the past week. The guy, Richard, claimed to be eighty-two, but he looked even older. *Do people,* Logan had said to the group, drawing a laugh, *still lie about their age at eighty-two? I mean,* he'd gone on, *at eighty-two he's still thirty-eight years older than her!* He'd noticed Melody watching him intently while he spoke, and he had half expected her to stay after to talk to him—she'd looked interested in that way, as if there was something she was relating to in his ranting—but she left as soon as the meeting ended. During one of his shares, Logan had made a joke about the black minivan he'd gotten stuck with by his rental car company. He found Melody's note pinned under its windshield wipers.

Logan checked his cell phone and saw that he was a little early, that it wasn't quite seven yet. He scanned the shadowy spaces under the pier and saw Melody leaning against a piling, pressed flat against it, as if she were trying to hide. She was wearing sandals and khaki shorts and a blue halter top, and he wouldn't have recognized her as the girl from the AA meeting except for the black hair and the straight line of bangs. While he was watching, she slid down the piling and sat in the sand, her legs stretched out in front of her. Logan had gone to bed assuming he would ignore her note, and then he had gotten up in the morning at six, as usual, and had his coffee, and started out for The Strand and the pier. He liked to be out of the house before seven anyway, when Becky got up, and he'd been taking this walk along The Strand in the mornings—but before he'd even made it partly down the Thirty-fourth Street hill he had decided he would meet Melody. He didn't think it could hurt anything, and maybe—who knew?—

there might be some way he could be of help to her. That was one of the things about AA. You were all supposed to be there for each other. So, here he was. He watched her for another moment, and then made his way down the beach and out onto the sand.

Melody saw him before he reached her. She had just pulled herself to her feet and started in on some yogalike stretches, and when she caught sight of him she backed away a few feet into the shadows, slid her hands into the pockets of her shorts, and watched him, her eyes fast on his eyes. Without all the makeup—the raccoon eyes were gone—and without the slinky dress and the stockings and the platform heels, she looked younger. She looked almost like all the other well-off teenagers he saw hanging out all day in town and on the beach—except for the black hair and the crazy neon nose thing she was still wearing. In the daylight, the little button hanging out her nostril seemed to move with each breath. It appeared to be a little fan of some sort, with tiny blades that turned as she breathed.

When he was standing in front of her, he said, "Okay, first thing I've got to ask is, what is that?" And he pointed to the nose stud and the dangling button.

"Firefly," she said. She pressed a finger against her left nostril and breathed out onto the button, making its tiny blades spin. "Some guy in Israel invented it supposedly." She touched the button. "It's like a little turbine. My breath generates enough electricity to keep the LED glowing." She smiled. "Cool, huh?"

Logan said, "Unbelievably cool," and then leaned back to look her over. The skin of her face, even without makeup, was flawless—a testament, he guessed, to the creams and lotions and medical care available to families with money. In comparison to some of the pockmarked and acne-ruined faces of the problem kids in

Saltwell, Melody was a goddess. "So," he said, and he lifted her note halfway out of his pocket. "How can I help you, Melody?"

"Can I explain some stuff to you first?" she asked. She looked out toward the beach on both sides of the pier. Behind Logan, a couple of surfers in wet suits were walking to the water, boards under their arms. "Can we go back here to talk?" she asked, and she pointed toward the shadows where the pier met the land. When Logan gave her a searching look, she said, "You're a cop. I'm not going to, like, have somebody waiting to mug you."

The thought hadn't even occurred to Logan. This wasn't the setup for a mugging. "I wasn't worried," he said. "But I don't think it would be a good idea for us to head back under the pier where the teens make out, whatever it is you have in mind."

She offered Logan a flirty smile, the kind of flirty smile typical of very young girls who hardly know what they're doing. "No one makes out under the pier," she said. "Must be another generation."

"Must be," Logan said, and he touched her back, directing her out into the sunlight. "Tell me," he said, "What's up?" He stretched, reaching for the sky. "Why did you ask me to meet you here? And," he added, "I'm an ex-cop. Didn't I say that? I'm retired."

"Aren't cops always cops?"

"Maybe," Logan said, and then was quiet and waited for her to answer his questions.

Melody, though, was taking her time. She walked alongside him in silence all the way across the beach up to The Strand. She didn't say a word until they were passing through a pair of pale blue gates, heading toward the coffee shop at the end of the pier. Then, as if they had been chatting all along, she said, "Your sister, she's like my stepmother's clone. Swear to God."

"How's that?" They were among a dozen people strolling along the pier, with maybe another dozen leaning against light blue railings, looking out over the beach or the ocean. The sun was bright already and hot.

"She's twenty-four, Cynthia, my stepmother—but she was twenty-two, like your sister, when she married my dad—and she married him, totally obviously, for his money, just like your sister married the first guy."

Logan said, "I don't think it was all about money with Becky." As soon as he spoke, a little shock of surprise startled him. Outside of AA meetings, he generally didn't talk about personal stuff with anyone, let alone sixteen-year-olds—and yet here he was, and it felt pretty comfortable at that. "She met him working as an extra on a movie. They were doing some location shooting in the mountains, and she got hired because she's gorgeous—"

"Cynthia too. Fashion model."

"Jack—ironic, same name as our father—was a friend of one of the producers. He seemed glamorous, and he lived on the other side of the country, which, that alone probably would have done it for her."

"And you think if he made minimum wage she would have married him?"

Logan thought about the question. "Okay," he said, finally. "You have a point."

"Look." Melody stopped and leaned against the railing. "Here's the story," she said, as if she was all of a sudden done with any fooling around. "I have to go back to my house, because all my stuff is there and I need my things."

"And?"

"And I'm afraid to go back there alone."

"You want me to go back to your house with you?"

"You're a cop. I thought—"

"So you're not living there now?"

"Sort of." She pushed her hair off her face and looked away a moment, as if trying to figure out how to explain. "So we had this big fight yesterday and yadda yadda yadda, I left. I spent the night at The Shade."

"The Shade?"

"Local hotel."

"Does your father know that? Does he know where you are?"

"His credit card," she said, looking across the pier, away from Logan. "Plus, it's happened before. He can find me."

"But he hasn't been in touch with you?" Logan asked. "He hasn't called to see if you're okay?"

Melody smirked. She looked like she wanted to say something but was holding back.

Logan said, "What was the fight about?"

"Money." Melody stared out over the sand before turning to look at Logan. "I threatened to sue him and he flipped out." She pulled up her hair and turned so that Logan could see a bruise and an ugly welt across the back of her neck. "He knocked me down and I hit the back of my head and my neck on the kitchen table."

Logan pushed her hair back to get a better look at the welt. It was ugly but nothing serious. "Has that happened before?"

Melody shook her head and then corrected herself. "I mean, yes, it's happened before, but that's not the big thing." She shrugged as if the physical violence was nothing. "The problem," she said, "is Cynthia." She took a breath, as if getting ready to explain something complicated. "Dad's put a lot of my money—money my grandparents left me—in custodial accounts. Now all of a sudden, Cynthia, who hasn't had a job since they got married, she's starting up her own modeling agency. Dad, I know, is already maxed out up to his ears with this other big thing he's got going on—trust me, too much to explain—so where's the money coming from? They can't touch my trust account, and that only leaves my UTMAs. So I'm like, Can I see my custodial accounts, please? I don't even know how much is in them, except I know it's a lot. And he's like, It's up to me what I do with that money. So I'm, You mean you can invest my money in Cynthia's business? And he goes, If I want to, yes. I'm, Okay fine, how about if I take you to court for stealing my money? And then he looks at me like he might kill me and goes, You know how much money your mother stole from me? The two of you, you're a pair of selfish bitches. So I told him to go fuck himself and that's when he hit me." She ran her fingers through her hair, as if calming herself. "I'm done with all his bullshit," she said. "Really. I can live on my own another year till I'm done with high school, and then I go to college and that's that. I won't have to deal with any of it."

Logan said, "You think you have enough money in those accounts to live on your own?"

Melody smiled, as if amused by the question. "Look," she said, "I'll pay you. The house is usually empty between eight and ten, and I could do it alone, except I really am afraid of what might happen if he caught me breaking into his study, which is what I have to do to get into my accounts."

Logan said, "Why do you need to break in to his study?"

"Because that's where he keeps his computer."

"Why do you need his computer to get to your accounts?"

"Because he keeps the passwords hidden on his computer, and he keeps the computer locked up in his study."

"So how do you plan on getting into his study if he keeps it locked?"

"That's where I was hoping you could help."

Logan laughed and a woman in matching red jogging shorts and halter top turned to look at him and then at Melody. She had been walking down the middle of the pier with her hands on her hips, probably cooling down after a run, and she looked at Logan and Melody as if trying to figure out the relationship before moving on, falling back into her own thoughts. Once she had passed, Logan said to Melody, "You want me to break in to your father's study for you? Is that what you're asking?"

"And be there to protect me if I get caught. Truly," she said, "I'm afraid of what he might do if he caught me."

Logan said, "I can't do that, Melody. I'm sorry. I could wind up in jail."

"Really? Even though you're a cop? Wouldn't that be like—"

"Cops wind up in jail all the time," Logan said. "To begin with. Next, I'm an ex-cop. And I'm an ex-cop from a small town in Virginia. Believe me, honey, that's not going to count for a whole hell of a lot in L.A."

"All right," Melody said. She hooked her arms over the railing and settled back, as if getting ready to negotiate. "What if you just come with me and you don't break into anything? Where's the risk in that?"

"Unless your father comes home and I wind up in a tussle with him."

"Then you'd be protecting me. That's not illegal."

"Okay," Logan said, "but what good does it do you to go back to your house if you can't get at his computer?"

"I can at least get some of my stuff."

"And for that," Logan said, "you don't need me."

"Unless he didn't lock up the study because I'm not in the house. I mean," she said, "that's a long shot, but—"

Logan laughed and said, "You're persistent. I'll give you that."

Melody leaned out over the railing and looked down to the beach. When Logan touched her back she said, "Forget it. I'm sorry I troubled you."

"Melody," Logan said, and then he couldn't find words. She looked lost, leaning over the pier, gazing down at nothing. He moved next to her and took up the same position.

Melody said, "I thought you'd understand. Cynthia's using my father to steal my money, and I'm like, because I'm sixteen, I'm powerless. I mean, I can go to court, yes, but all I need to do is get at his computer and once I have his passwords, I can transfer the money into my personal accounts, where he can't get at it. Then that's it. It's done and I'm out of there, and I'm fine until I'm eighteen and I can get at my trust."

"Can you really do that?" Logan asked. "Transfer from the custodial accounts to personal accounts? I mean doesn't that all have to be set up with routing numbers and authentications and all that?"

"That's all done," Melody said, a little note of hope coming back into her voice. "He already transfers money into my accounts every few months. Only, you know, a few hundred to a few thousand at a time. And they're all my accounts. It's all my money."

Logan said, "Just how much is in these accounts, Melody?"

Again, Melody didn't answer.

"What?" Logan said. "Are you afraid I'm going to charge too much?"

"Will you do it?" Melody asked. "Please."

Logan looked across the pier out onto the sand, where a pair of young women in identical one-piece bright red bathing suits were hitting a volleyball softly back and forth over a net. "What made you ask me?" he said. "What made you think I'd help?"

"Like I said, I thought you'd understand because of your sister." Melody joined him in looking across the pier. "And, I don't know, just something about you."

Logan echoed her. "Just something about me . . ." He added, as it occurred to him, "And where is your mother in all this?"

"Who?"

"Your mother."

"Oh," Melody said, "her. She's in Paris."

Logan said, "Doesn't she have any say—"

"Can we please not talk about my mother, please? Trust me, she's a nightmare. She's a heartless, untrustworthy thief and a liar. If she ever gets in touch with me or Dad it's because she wants money. That's it." Melody threw her head back and closed her eyes, as if taking a moment to compose herself, and about the time Logan thought she was done, she started up again. "That's my relationship with my mother, how much money she can squeeze out of my accounts. Beyond that, she has no use for me—and I stopped having any use for her a long time ago. So my mother is not a part of the story, okay? We can just drop the subject."

"Subject's dropped," Logan said, and he was surprised to see that Melody's eyes were brimming. Her tone had been cold and maybe angry, but not tearful. She turned around and blotted her eyes before gazing down at the sand. Logan touched her shoulder and said, "Look. Okay. I'll go with you back to your house. I'll sit at a table somewhere while you do whatever you do. If your father or anyone else shows up, I'm going to say we met at an AA meeting, you said that you had reason to be afraid to return to your house, and that you asked me to escort you because I'm an ex-cop. That's all I know. That's my whole story. You asked me to help because you feared for your personal safety, and I helped."

"Thank you," Melody said. She smiled and touched his arm, and in another moment she was beaming.

Logan added, as if talking to himself, "The welt on the back of your neck makes it plausible. So . . . I don't think I'm really taking much of a risk."

Melody watched Logan, as if curious about something, and then her smile turned coy. "I knew you'd do it," she said. "Soon as I saw you."

"You did?" Logan said. "And how's that?"

"I could tell."

Logan gave her a look that said he didn't know what she was talking about. "So where do you live?" he asked.

Melody pointed to The Strand. "That big modern stone and polished-wood monster," she said. "The one that takes up half the block."

"Really?" The place she was pointing at was only a couple of blocks away. If it sold for less than twenty million he'd be shocked.

"Really." Melody gave Logan a quick hug and then took his hand and pulled him out onto the pier.

Standing at the entrance to a huge living room, all white walls and track lighting, contemporary art, paintings, sculptures, stone floors, leather couches and lounges, a wet bar, a line of windows and glass doors leading out to decks that overlooked the ocean, Logan couldn't help but be a little stunned by the conspicuousness of the wealth evident in everything from the quality of the furnishings to the luxury of abundant space. The closest he had ever come before to the interior of a place like this was in his dentist's office while browsing an issue of *Architectural Digest.*

Melody seemed annoyed as he stopped upon entering the room, but then she softened as she noticed the look in his eyes. "Yes," she said, gazing over the room herself, as if confirming its splendor. "But trust me," she added, "growing up here was like growing up in a mausoleum."

Logan said, "A luxurious mausoleum."

"True," Melody said, and she took his hand and squeezed it, and then leaned against him and rested her head on his shoulder. "But still a mausoleum," she said, and looked over the room as if what she saw wounded her, and she needed Logan for solace.

For Logan, upon entering that living room, the situation changed in a way that at first confused him—and then he realized he felt like an intruder, which, he reasoned, shouldn't really surprise him since that was exactly the case. He pointed to one of the brown leather sofas in the center of the room. "I'll wait here," he said. "You go get your stuff."

Melody gave Logan a quick tight hug and then scurried away across the living room and disappeared down one of the wide, seemingly endless, hallways.

Logan sat on one of the sofas, letting himself sink back into the slick cushion, but he was on his feet again after a few seconds, unable to sit still. He went to the line of windows and looked out over the beach and ocean, at the surfers and kayakers and paddleboarders and, off in the distance, a sleek white boat skimming over the blue-gray water. He stood in the heat of an intense morning sun that penetrated the windows and washed over the cool, perfectly air-conditioned room, and he thought about the stifling summer heat of the run-down clapboard tin-roofed house where he grew up, where the nearest escape from the heat was a swimming hole in the aptly named nearby Poverty Creek. He thought of weeks when there wasn't enough food because Big Jack had gambled and whored and drank away his paycheck; he thought of his mother tending to his cuts and bruises; and he thought of him and Becky tending to their mother's cuts and bruises, and he thought about Big Jack, that lumbering hulk of a man everyone in Saltwell, Virginia, seemed to love and everyone in his own family loathed and feared. He saw him in his Sunday best, taking the family to church, looking clean and decent in a pressed blue suit with his dark hair parted on the right and slicked back unnaturally neat, and he saw him passed out in the cab of his truck with a bottle of Wild Turkey empty on the seat beside him—and when Logan finally turned around and again looked over the immaculately clean stone floors and white walls of Melody's living room, he felt a little shaky, and he wasn't sure why.

He started for the wet bar, meaning to pour himself a glass of water, when he heard wood cracking and breaking, followed by a loud pop and snap, and then a furious hammering, and he laughed because he knew even before he followed the hallway to the source of the racket that Melody was trying to break in to her father's study, and was likely at that moment working at smashing through the door with a large blunt object—which, when he rounded a corner and saw what he had accurately guessed he would see, was a crowbar.

"I've almost got it," Melody said. She was sweating and there were tears in her eyes. In the way she was crouched by the door, in the look on her face, there was something desperate and pained and close to defeat. It was a look he had seen before.

Logan took the crowbar from her. The door was solid wood with a deadbolt over a brass doorknob. Melody had managed to loosen the hinges but beyond that hadn't made much progress. Logan slammed his foot into the bottom right corner of the door, jammed the crowbar into the tiny wedge of space Melody had opened near the hinges, and then kicked and pried the door off the bottom hinge first and then the upper hinge. When he lifted the door out of its frame and leaned it against the wall, Melody hugged him around the neck, kissed him on the lips, and then jumped for a cherrywood desk situated in front of a shaded window. She immediately fired up a desktop Macintosh computer, and when it issued the familiar Mac chime as it booted up, she said, "This won't take me fifteen minutes, I swear."

Logan took a few steps into the study and thought about sitting in one of the two black leather chairs that were in a corner alcove facing a pair of sliding glass doors that led out to a secluded corner deck. In the study proper, the shades were all drawn. The sunlight that filled the room and spilled over the blond hardwood floor came in through the glass doors and the alcove. "Is that your father?" Logan asked. He was standing by a photograph of a man in his late forties, early fifties, with his arm around a woman half his age, who looked like she could indeed be a fashion model.

Melody pulled herself away from the computer to look at the photograph. "Dad and the bitch," she confirmed. She waved her arm to indicate the half dozen other framed pictures here and there around the study, perched on ledges or on a pair of console tables. "Notice," she said, "the pictures of me all over," and then she went immediately back to her work on the computer.

Logan scanned all the pictures and saw only the father and the new wife and an assortment of older people.

"Here they are," Melody said, and laughed. "He's such an idiot."

Logan said, "His passwords?"

Without looking up from the computer, Melody said, "He has them listed on a sticky note," and then repeated herself, "What an idiot."

While Melody's fingers tapped away at the keyboard, Logan leaned over to get a closer look at Cynthia, the young wife. She had long blonde hair, deeply tanned skin, and dark eyes. She looked alert and smart and full of a good health that radiated out of the picture. At home, in Saltwell, in his apartment's spare bedroom that served as a den, he kept his parents' wedding photograph in a frame—and in that photograph Cicy, his mother, radiated the same youth and good health, and she was every bit as beautiful as Melody's fashion-model stepmother, though it was of course a simpler beauty. Remembering his mother's wedding picture, how beautiful she was in her white gown, made him recall her at the time of her death, when he was seventeen and she wasn't quite forty: haggard, unhealthily skinny, her face etched with the lines and creases of a much older woman, and that nasty scar under her left eye, a gift from her husband.

"Done," Melody said. "Piece of cake," and she looked up beaming at Logan. "By the time they figure out what happened, they won't be able to do a damn thing about it."

"Good," Logan said. "Are we out of here, then?"

"No hurry." Melody glanced down at the computer, apparently checking the time. "We still have a couple of hours before Rosa shows."

"Rosa?"

"Come on," Melody said, not bothering with his question. "Let's celebrate." She shut down the computer, wiped the keyboard and desktop clean with the bottom of her dress, and then hurried past him, out of the study and down the hall.

Logan's gaze settled on the computer, his attention stuck on Melody wiping down the keyboard.

"Hey!" Melody's voice came from down the hallway. "Are you coming?"

Logan looked from the computer to the nearby photograph of Cynthia smiling, and then exited the room through the busted-out doorway.

He found Melody in what was obviously her bedroom. The white comforter on her bed was tossed back, and she was stretched out on black silk sheets with her head over a teak end table where she had laid out four fat lines of coke on a mirror. She beamed up at him. "Time to celebrate," she said. She snorted a line with a rolled-up bill, threw her head back, and offered the bill to Logan as she fell over onto a row of black pillows.

Logan took the bill and crossed the room to stand in front of a wall of shaded windows. Through the shades he could see the darkened beach and ocean. "Why did you wipe down the keyboard?" he asked. "Are you worried about fingerprints?" He turned around to find her naked except for a bright red thong. Against the black sheets her skin was white as a flare.

"What do you care?" she said, and she clasped her hands behind her head, showing off her body in a way that was both a parody of sexiness and the real thing.

Logan said, "You wouldn't be stealing money from your father, would you?"

Melody smiled coyly, as if to suggest that might indeed be the case. "Trust me, Logan," she said, "if I'm stealing from him, he deserves it." She found another bill in the night table drawer, snorted a second line of coke, and collapsed on the bed, her arms flung wide, her hands clasping the black sheets. She seemed to drift away, and when she came back she said, dreamily, "Come here, Logan." She said it as if she knew him intimately and knew he would come to her.

When Logan knelt on the bed, leaned over Melody, and snorted the two lines of coke one right after the other, it hit him like walking through a doorway into a smoky room, a space clouded in a familiar, comfortable haze. He grunted as if affirming the pleasure that washed over him, and then he kissed Melody gently, blindly, his eyes closed, feeling for her neck, her cheek, making his way to her lips. When he opened his eyes, she was watching him, her own eyes dazed and yet still touched with something fiery. She returned his gentle kiss with a bite, and then she clawed at his back and shoulders, her sharp nails pushing under his shirt to get at skin. In another moment he was naked and a little dizzy as he kissed Melody, trying to crawl up into her, through her mouth, through her eyes, while someone was moaning, he couldn't be sure who, it might have been coming from either one of them, that animal-like lowing, that keening that seemed all at once to be everywhere.

Jekyll Island

CHARLOTTE SAYS I'M EVOLVED. ME, I THINK I'M ABOUT AS evolved as the alligator I saw this morning floating lazily along a canal, its armor-scaled back and pop-up eyes drifting in front of the surprisingly graceful slow swish of its tail. We're in Georgia, on Jekyll Island. It's August and hot, temperature over 100 every day so far. We're staying on the north end of the beach, in a condominium complex called Villas by the Sea. At night, I stand on the balcony and watch the weather over the ocean until I feel like I might be able to sleep. Then I slip into bed with Char, and lay awake a little longer in the dark. Across the hall, I hear footsteps in Jonathan's room, sometimes the tinny leakage of music from his earbuds. He must play it at a deafening volume. Jonathan appears never to sleep. He's up at night, he's up in the middle of the night, he's up in the morning when I take my coffee across the road and walk a quarter mile along a dirt path, braving mosquitoes and black flies, for a look at the sleepy canal, where I've seen terrapins, an alligator, a snowy egret, woodpeckers, myriad fish sunning themselves in the shallows.

Jonathan's vacationing with us for a week before he leaves to finish his tour in Iraq. Charlotte's forty, fifteen years older than Jonathan, and I'm fifty-five, fifteen years older than Charlotte.

Burning Man

We're like a ladder with big fifteen-year steps, and me at the top. Jonathan's my son and Charlotte's my girlfriend. Charlotte thinks I'm evolved because I love Jonathan regardless of his choices, like joining the Marines and going to war. I'm against the war in Iraq. I think it's a crime. But I don't fight with Jonathan. I don't argue with him. In the week and a half we've been together on this island, there's been no mention of Iraq. We don't watch television. We're not reading the papers. In the morning, we all share a pleasant breakfast; then we spend the day on the beach, or bicycling when we can bear the heat, or reading in the air-conditioning, taking our view of the ocean through hurricane-proof plate glass. When one of us sees dolphins, or a fishing boat, or a sea kayaker skimming elegantly over the water, we go out on the balcony, share the binoculars, and talk about the view. This morning we watched a line of pelicans flying so low their wings almost touched their own shadows on the water. I love Georgia's coastal islands. I've vacationed here before with Jonathan, but when Charlotte and I planned this trip, he wasn't included. It's luck we had the second bedroom. Jonathan called and said he was coming home on leave, and we invited him to come along with us.

 He relaxes a little more each day. I can see it in the way he holds his shoulders, and I can see it in his eyes. A month before this leave, two of his buddies were killed in a helicopter crash. When he told us on the phone, he didn't mention that he was on the helicopter too. We found out a few days later. This leave is probably related to that crash, but he's not talking and I'm not asking. Physically, he looks as healthy as young men get. He's on the tall side at six foot, a good two inches taller than me. He gets the height from his mother's side of the family, where all the men are six foot or taller. His mother died when he was two, in an auto accident everyone knows was suicide, including Jonathan. Though I never told him, not directly. When he was seventeen, after his high school graduation party, after spending the day with family, including his mother's family, he found me sitting alone in the garden behind our house. I was sitting in a lawn chair, using a second chair as a foot rest. I had built an artificial pond back there, and I was admiring my work, watching a broad trickle of water drop down a series of slate steps into a pool with goldfish and koi. Jonathan pulled a chair up alongside me and stared at the water a long while before he said, "Mom's car hit a bridge abutment at over a hundred miles an hour, and there were no skid marks, Dad. Is that right?" I knew what he was asking. I said, "Yes. That's right." He put his arm around my back, and we both went on watching the trickle of water in silence, until one of his friends called him away.

I never remarried. Jonathan went off to college in New York, at NYU, and the careful, well-managed life I had arranged for him promptly unraveled. In New York, he got into every kind of trouble a young man can get into. He dropped out of school after two years. He worked a hodgepodge of crappy jobs, never lasting more than a few months at any of them. He found one loser girlfriend after another, some of them . . . Jesus. I don't know where he found them. One girl I met when I traced him to an apartment in Crown Heights—this after not having heard from him in more than six months and going half crazy with worry. I knocked on the door, sick just from the sight of the place, the stink of urine in the halls, the front door busted up and looking like it had recently been kicked open. A slovenly woman opened the door. She looked like someone out of a Diane Arbus photo. She must have been twice Jonathan's age. At least. When Jonathan came to the door, he was sweaty and feverish and unsteady on his feet. He couldn't have weighed much more than a hundred pounds. I took him from there to a hospital, and from a hospital to home, where he stayed with me for three months, until he was healthy enough to go back to New York, where the cycle of disasters started all over again. So when I see him now, standing on the balcony in bathing trunks, his torso lean and muscular as an Olympic swimmer, his body bronzed and glistening, I'm grateful. He's healthy, and that's what matters to me. Yes, I hate the war in Iraq. Yes, I believe the war is criminal. And I don't care. As long as my son is healthy. Forgive me if I don't feel particularly evolved.

Though he has largely kept to himself for most of the week, Jonathan has not been unsociable. He talks easily during meals, and he's friendly to Charlotte. Friendlier to her, it seems, than he is to me. Charlotte is thin, with cascading curly black hair that flies out from her head in waves, ripples past her shoulders, down to the middle of her back. She's quiet and can be sullen at times, and always she seems at least a little unhappy—and it is largely true that she is usually at least a little unhappy. The romantics would have called her a melancholic. I'm supposed to be an engineer, but really I've been in management for the past dozen years. I make a good living at my work, though I lost any serious interest in it years ago. These days my interests are history and literature, especially the romantics, which is how I met Charlotte. I took her course in romantic poetry. She teaches at a branch college outside Alexandria, Virginia, where I live. At the end of the semester, after the last class, I waited till the other students were gone, and then I went around to the side of her desk and said, trying for an amused tone, "Now that I'm not your student, would you consider having dinner with me this weekend?" We had gotten along well all semester. She had relied on me to get the class conversation moving, and she seemed to be impressed with my knowledge of the era. I don't know what I expected. She was, I thought then and still think, an extraordinarily attractive woman, and I knew she was a lot younger than me, so I was prepared for a polite rejection. I didn't, however, expect the look of fury that came over her face, as if she were thinking about slapping me, and then I was even more surprised when that look dissolved into something closer to fear and she said, sounding unsure, "Okay," and nodded her head. That's the way she is. It's as if, sometimes, having to speak at all, at least person to person, at least initially, angers her, or scares her half to death. Of course, once she gets to know someone, it's easier. She talks a little easier. But, as I say, she seems always at least a little unhappy, and she's always reserved. So when she and Jonathan got along comfortably from the start, I was first amazed and then grateful.

I was with Charlotte for several months before I learned she was bisexual. She was concerned about telling me, worried it might scare me away. Apparently, she had been moving between men and women all her life, from the time she was fifteen. Her first sexual relationship was with a girl, in her junior year of high school. In her senior year, she dated a guy. Then in her first year of college she was with a girl, and in her second year she was with a guy, and she went back and forth like that until she got married, to a guy, in her late twenties. The marriage lasted ten years. She had two children with her husband before she left him—for a woman. That lasted a little more than a year—and then came me. We've been seeing each other for two years now, and—though it surprises both of us equally—the relationship keeps getting deeper and better. Still, it took her months to tell me any of this—any of the stuff about the women in her life—so I nearly choked when she told Jonathan about it on the first night of the vacation, when they had known each other for all of a few hours.

The circumstances of that first night were dramatic—which probably explains some of it. We had arrived at our condo early in the evening, and after unpacking and eating a thrown-together meal, we all three went for a walk along the beach. The tide was coming in, leaving only a thin strip of white sand. We followed a wooden walkway over the dunes in moonlight, past a gazebo where a young couple lay side by side looking out at the ocean, holding hands across a pair of white plastic lounge chairs. The beach was just wide enough for the three of us to walk abreast, though I was in the ocean up to my ankles. There were no waves to speak of, just a lazy slight rise and fall of water, waves you could measure in millimeters. Again we made a kind of ladder in height, only with me in the middle, a couple of inches taller than Charlotte, and Jonathan at the top. Charlotte seemed instantly relaxed by the beach and the water and the moonlight. She walked between us. We were all barefoot—we had left our shoes and sandals on the gazebo. We were wearing shorts and T-shirts. I was the old man in this trio, and I would not have been shocked had a stranger assumed Jonathan and Charlotte were the couple. I was still managing to look fairly youthful, though. In general, people didn't seem surprised when they saw that Charlotte and I were together.

We were talking about the ocean, how beautiful it is and the feeling of serenity that seemed to rise up out of such an expanse of water, when I saw what looked like a piece of driftwood floating near the shore. In the moonlight, it looked like a long blue-black hump in the dark water, bobbing lazily in the surf. When I took a few hurried steps toward it, meaning to push it out of our way, it rose up, turned slightly toward me, and I saw it was an alligator. Then it made a sudden movement, turning itself parallel to the shore so it was facing me. Before I could gather myself to say anything, Jonathan had me by the arm and Charlotte's hands were on my back, and together they pulled and pushed me out of the water, both of them laughing, though Jonathan's laughter sounded mostly surprised while Charlotte's was more shocked.

I said, "What the hell's an alligator doing in the ocean?" I felt as if some cosmic rule had been violated.

Jonathan said, "That's new. Never seen that before."

We had climbed up a dune, and we saw that someone else, walking along the beach in the opposite direction, was already on her cell phone. We could see her in the moonlight, standing on the rocks fifty feet away from us. She must have heard our shouting and seen us scramble up the dune. She held up the cell phone to us, yelled out "I called the Park Authority," and then took a seat on the rocks to watch the gator. Ten minutes later, a truck drove up behind the dunes and two young rangers got out carrying poles designed to lasso gators, and then another truck arrived a minute later with a big cage. It took them half an hour of wrangling to get the gator in the cage, and before they were done there were a dozen of us on the dunes and rocks watching the show.

At one point, when the young woman wielding the pole-lasso waded knee-deep in the surf, perilously close to the big gator, Charlotte said to Jonathan, "I used to date a woman who worked as a park ranger."

Jonathan said "Where?" without missing a beat, as if there

was nothing unusual about my girlfriend having once dated a woman.

"Montana," Charlotte said, and then went on with a story about her girlfriend and an isolated fire-watch station in the wilds.

Jonathan said he had a buddy in Iraq who once did the very same kind of work, only he was stationed in a high tower up in the Sawtooth Mountains with a view that extended for a hundred miles.

Charlotte had something to say in response to that, and then the two of them were off on an easy conversation about nature and wilderness, and I heard Jonathan explain—to my surprise, never having heard anything like it from him before—that he'd love to work in the wilderness, alone in a watchtower, with nothing to do but look at trees and mountains and maybe read a good book when he got tired of staring off into the distances.

When the rangers' work was done, the gator caged in the back of a truck, and the trucks driving off toward the road, Charlotte asked me if that was the strangest thing I'd ever seen on the island. Jonathan and I exchanged a glance Charlotte didn't notice.

Jonathan said, "Remember the time we saw that deer on the beach?"

I did remember. Jonathan was a boy, maybe ten years old. We were with some good friends that year, and it was me and Jonathan and my friend's wife, Marcella. We had a house on the beach and were out on the deck watching a fat orange moon hanging over the ocean when a deer ambled down to the water and looked up at the moon for all the world like it was admiring the sight. It stayed there a good while, still and quiet, just looking out over the water.

Charlotte asked a question about the deer, and then the

talk moved on. The look Jonathan and I exchanged was about another incident, one neither one of us, apparently, wanted to explain. It was the same vacation with the deer. I had gotten up early to watch the sunrise and found Jonathan already up waiting for me. I had said the night before that I planned on taking a sunrise walk on the beach. He must have set his alarm. On our walk that morning, with the sun still low on the horizon, we saw a half dozen people moving very slowly down to the beach, hauling something carefully between them in a dark blue blanket they were carrying like a sling, one on each corner, two in the middle on each side. We were approaching the procession as it moved slowly toward the surf, and I exchanged a look with a couple of the men—there were three men and three women, all young, maybe in their thirties, and I guessed they were couples—and the look seemed to me as full of sorrow as a human look gets. Then I saw they were carrying a terribly wasted human figure in the sling. Her hair was matted and cut short, but still I could see it was the face of a young woman. She was lifting her head with great effort, trying to look out at the ocean. Her arms were nothing more than bones with some pallid flesh stuck to them. The skull beneath her face was horribly evident. Jonathan saw her too, and he stopped and wrapped his arms around my waist. I put my hand on his back and moved him on past the procession, which had reached the water and was carefully lowering the blanket on one side, trying to give the woman a better view. I explained to Jonathan that the woman was very likely dying and had probably asked her friends to let her see the ocean one last time. When I looked down to Jonathan I saw he had a distant, faraway look. He didn't say anything and neither did I. I put my hand on his shoulder and we finished our walk. Every once in a while since then, one or the other of us would bring it up, but neither of us ever had a lot to say about it.

I have a tattoo of a starfish on the fleshy fold of skin between my thumb and forefinger. It's small, less than an inch in diameter. It has a black border and bright red edges that shade to yellow in the center, creating the illusion of depth. Midway through the vacation, Jonathan and I took a sunset walk together along the beach, and he asked me about the tattoo. He knows the story. I got the tattoo soon after his mother died. She grew up on Ocracoke Island, where she'd scour the beaches for starfish. She loved those memories. She talked about them all the time.

I said, "It's a way of remembering Alanna." Then I looked at him and said, "You knew that."

"What I meant," he said, "was why on your hand, where you have to look at it all the time, where you can't really get away from it?"

I didn't know what to say to that. I hadn't thought about it that way. I remembered thinking when I got it that I wanted something about her to remain with me, physically, as a part of my body.

Before I could try to explain, Jonathan said, "Warren had a tattoo of a red cardinal on his shoulder. Everybody busted his balls about it, 24/7."

Warren was one of his buddies who died in the crash. I asked Jonathan what was wrong with a cardinal tattoo, and he gave me a look like I was from another planet. "Not really a Marine-type tattoo," he said. "He took all kinds of shit for it. It was big." He pointed to his bicep. "Right there. Bright red." He looked down at my starfish, which was also bright red. "But he could keep the thing covered most of the time."

I put my arm around his shoulder, but then took it away quickly when I felt him tighten up. "So what are you saying, Jonathan? You don't like my tattoo?"

"I was thinking of getting the same tattoo, a red cardinal, but I was thinking I'd get it in the same place, on my bicep—and now, seeing yours again, I'm thinking there's something about having it right in your face all the time, so you can't forget ever, not for a second."

I said, "That wasn't what I was thinking when I got it," and then neither of us said another word for the rest of the walk. We passed a stand of trees high up on the dunes. The crowns of the trees were pointed inland, and they looked like a big wind was blowing, pushing back every leaf and branch, but they had grown that way in response to the wind and weather that came in off the ocean. I wanted to comment on the trees, but said nothing. Later, on Driftwood Beach, where the sand is covered with a small forest of washed-up trees, we passed a sea turtle nest, and I wanted to remind Jonathan of the time we'd watched a huge sea turtle lumber across this beach. It had been a gorgeous late evening, right after sunset. The kids had been climbing on the trees when one of them spotted the turtle. It was me and Jonathan and Marcella's girls, Iris and Carla. The kids were dancing and shouting with excitement, cheering the turtle on across the beach. It was a wonderful memory. But I didn't say anything.

Once we were back in the apartment, Jonathan started up the stairs and then stopped after a couple of steps. "Dad," he said, "I've got six more months, and then I'm done with Iraq. I'm done with the Marines."

What I might have said to him on that walk: all the things he doesn't know. All the secrets Alanna kept for me. That I ran around on her, that I was irresponsible, that I gambled away our money, that I was a drunk. That the morning he was born I was in bed with a girl I had picked up at a bar the night before. That she was barely of age, and that she cried when she woke up and realized she had spent the night with me. That when I left the house the night before he was born, I promised Alanna I'd only be gone an hour. She was already having contractions when I left. I remember the look on her face, like she couldn't believe I was going out and why did she ever expect anything different? I should have told him that I humiliated her, again and again, before he was born and after. If I started with the stories, I don't know where I'd stop. The time she found a used condom in our bed, when she and I were trying to have a baby. The multiple times women called the house looking for me. The times I lost our grocery money at the track. The times I lost our rent money. How cruel I could be to her. How mean. How I loved her and felt trapped and smothered by loving her. How I wished she would leave me, how I pushed her and pushed her.

    I don't know why I did any of it. I didn't know why I was doing it when I was doing it. There was something in me uncontrollable then.

    I was stupid. I was young.

    Nothing explains it.

    I might have told him all of these things. One day, when the timing is better, I will.

Charlotte and Jonathan are in the condo packing, getting ready to leave, and I'm out at the canal with a cup of coffee. I scared off the gator when I approached the bank and watched it swim away. Jonathan will spend a few more days with me before he flies back to Iraq. Charlotte is planning on moving in with me. She brought it up for the first time last night, and I heard myself say I thought it was a great idea. Often it's like that: I do or say something and then think about it later. Do I want Charlotte to live with me? I came out here, to the canal, to give myself a little time and space to think. Me and the gator. Me and the turtles. And while I should be thinking about Charlotte moving in with me or Jonathan going back to Iraq, I'm thinking instead about Alanna.

I'm thinking, Alanna's son is a Marine. Alanna and I, a couple of peaceniks going back to the Vietnam War—and our son is a Marine. And where is he fighting? In the worst war of our lifetime. He's smart and sensitive, always has been. How does that fit? What kind of sense does that make? And I'm thinking about me. I read poetry and history. I'm with a woman who teaches literature at a local college. I've been with her for two years and we've never once had a violent fight, nor are we likely to. And, oh, she's bisexual. If Alanna could hear me now, she'd be laughing. She wouldn't believe any of it. Nor would she believe that I haven't had a drink or placed a bet in more than twenty years, and that I'll never do either again. But I haven't and I won't.

There's a beach here where driftwood tumbles out of the ocean and arranges itself in scenes so beautiful they're like dreams. I've walked along that beach many times—and I've never walked there once without thinking of Alanna. She would have loved this place, where deer come down to the water's edge in moonlight and stare out over the ocean, where huge sea turtles come up out of the waves to lay eggs in the sand.

I've seen an alligator in the surf here, a dying woman hauled along the beach in a sling, and a deer looking out over the ocean under an orange moon. These images, this morning, are shuttling back and forth through my thoughts.

An alligator in the surf, a dying woman on the beach, a deer looking out over the ocean.

I have no idea what it means. I have no idea what will happen next.

The Athlete

IT HAD BEEN YEARS SINCE EL PLAYED A GAME OF CHESS ON AN actual chessboard with actual pieces, and even longer since he had chatted easily with a woman, and yet there he was, in the ornate living room of an old Victorian home in Lexington, Kentucky, seated in an overstuffed chair across from Tess, a tallish, athletic-looking woman of about his age, mid- to late fifties, though he'd have guessed when he first met her that she was younger. She sat across from him in a matching chair, looking down to the slate table between them at a handsome antique chessboard and pieces. She wore faded blue jeans and a thin pale orange turtleneck sweater that hid the loose folds of her neck, where, he had noticed the night before, her age did show. In her eyes he found a mix of intelligence and weariness he associated with successful women. He'd just explained that all the chess playing he'd done lately had been on a computer screen, with anonymous opponents from all over the world, and she'd said *huh*, as if it amazed her anyone would want to spend his time playing chess with someone he couldn't see. They'd been talking like this, sharing little bits and pieces of their lives, for the past day and a half, since they'd been seatmates on a flight out of New York to Roanoke, Virginia—a flight that had been diverted because of fog. They'd wound up in the Lexington airport late in the evening, and when flights there were grounded because of snow, they wound up sharing a cab to the same bed-and-breakfast a few miles from the airport, where they wound up sharing nightcaps in Tess's room, followed by more easy conversation that lasted for hours and ended with them making love and falling asleep in each other's arms.

In the morning, to El's surprise, there was very little awkwardness. They'd risen, showered, dressed, and then gone down to breakfast chattering away, talking about everything in the world, from their histories and their lives to politics and science. It was as if neither of them could talk fast enough. Turned out, they both lived in Tribeca, relatively close to each other: El on North Moore Street, Tess on Leonard. They were both divorced, El for six years, Tess for ten. El had been married for a dozen years before the divorce, Tess for more than twenty. They both had grown children: Tess, two girls and a boy; El, a son and a daughter. Tess worked in fund-raising, El was in sales.

After breakfast, they'd retired to the living room and spent most of the rest of the day in front of an open fireplace, and every hour or so one or the other of them took a chunk of wood from a stack on the red brick outer hearth and tossed it into the flames. When it was clear there would be no flights out of Lexington until sometime the next day, the woman who ran the B and B, a grandmotherly figure with a balding head of gray hair and a belly that made her look impossibly pregnant, asked if they'd mind if she left them alone for a while, while she went to look after an elderly friend. Now it was late afternoon, the light outside gray and solemn, and they were alone in the house, midway through a chess game neither of them cared much about, a game that was meant only to provide an occasional diversion from their ongoing conversation.

The Athlete

Tess looked up from the chessboard, out a bay window overlooking a sloping hill and a trail that disappeared into a line of snow-covered trees. "Let's go for a walk," she said, "before it gets dark."

"Seriously?" El looked out the window again, as if he might have been missing something. The snow was still coming down, though lightly, and there looked to be a foot or so on the ground. The scene was peaceful—gently falling snow over fields and woods—until a gust of wind sent furious white swirls spinning into the trees.

"You're a big guy," Tess said. "You can take it."

El said, "Looks awfully cold out there," and then opened his arms and gazed down at himself, at the thin, dressy slacks and black shoes, at the white cotton shirt with fine blue stripes, more appropriate for a board meeting than a hike in the snow.

"She's got everything," Tess said. She jumped up from her chair, as if officially announcing the game of chess was over. "Look at this." She opened a door off the foyer to reveal a closet stuffed full of winter gear in a variety of sizes: coats, scarves, boots, hats, gloves, multiples of everything. "Elwood," she said, using his full name, teasing a little. "They have actual real woods here in Kentucky. Right out there, in fact." She pointed out the bay window.

El wrapped a long green scarf around his neck and foraged among the winter coats, looking for something that might fit him. He was six-one and bulky, with thick legs and heavy thighs. "Did I tell you I played point guard in college?" he asked as he tried on the only coat he could find that would reach down to his waist.

"Really?" Tess said. "I love basketball. Were you good?" Then she added, quickly, "I mean, you must have been good—"

El laughed and said, "That's all right." He was struggling to get the coat zipper up over his belly. "I was too small to get much playing time, but when they let me on the court, I usually did pretty well."

"Did you like playing?"

"Loved it," El said, and left it at that. He took a step back and opened his arms. The coat was too small for him, but he'd managed to get it zipped up and buttoned.

"You need to put a second pair of pants on over those," she said. "Do you have anything a little sturdier?"

"Pants?" He shook his head. "I've got another pair of dress slacks."

"Better go get them," she said. "The wind will whip right through those; might as well be naked."

El said, "Fine. I'll be a well-dressed woodsman," and he went back up to the bedroom, where he found a heavier pair of socks and put them on over the first pair, and then struggled into a second pair of pants.

Before leaving the room, he looked at himself in a freestanding, full-length mirror. As he expected, he looked ridiculous: a big guy with a round face framed by a full head of gray hair, wearing a too-tight winter coat and a long green scarf with gray dress slacks, two pair. He smiled, amused at the figure he cut—and then his thoughts took a quick turn back to basketball. He had been modest with Tess. He hadn't told her that in high school he'd been the team's leading scorer sophomore through senior year, and that one college scout who watched him play said he had the sweetest three-point shot in the region. Still, he had no offers from Division I schools. Too small. He'd heard it over and over, through high school and college. Too small. After high school, he traveled halfway across the country to play for Oklahoma Wesleyan, a good Division II basketball school—only to get limited playing time, because, of course, he was too small to compete against the bigger, stronger players in the league.

Too small. The words were lodged somewhere deep inside him like slivers of heat. He told Tess he loved basketball, but his feeling for the game, back then at least, was something more than that. His whole life was immersed in basketball. When he wasn't playing, he was practicing. When he wasn't practicing the game, he was thinking about it. He did only what he had to do to get through the academics in high school, and the same in college. He was a good basketball player, and he believed that would be his future. In high school, he believed he'd be recruited by a Division I team and go on to play in the pros. When that didn't happen and he went on to a Division II school, he believed he'd be noticed there and go on to play in the pros. When that didn't happen, when he finished college having spent infinitely more time on the bench than on the court, he found himself ill-prepared for the work world. He wound up in sales by default, and he'd been in sales ever since. When he thought of basketball now, it was often with anger. His coaches and teammates, his parents and his friends, they'd all tried to tell him: he was too small for the pros. It wasn't going to happen. He'd never forgiven them for being right, nor himself for not proving them wrong. His memories of basketball were buried in him like flames, like a roiling circle of heat.

Downstairs, he found Tess in front of the bay window, bundled up in a red quilted ski jacket, a white knit cap with ear muffs, and a long green scarf identical to the one he was wearing. "You look like a Christmas tree," he said, and then laughed at his own joke.

"I put out some boots," Tess said. "They look like they'll fit you." She pointed to the closet.

El said, "perfect," as he slid his foot into a boot. A moment later he'd donned a knit cap and gloves and was heading out the front door with Tess behind him.

"Cold," Tess said, announcing the obvious. She pulled her hat down over her forehead and wrapped her scarf over her face so only her eyes were exposed.

They waited together on the front steps of the house, looking across a snow-covered slope that descended to a blacktop road. A plow had gone by less than an hour earlier, and the road was slushy with patches of ice and snow. Beyond the road was an open field surrounded by trees.

El said, "Sure you want to do this?"

Tess said, "I bet you it'll be warmer when we get into the trees and out of the wind," and then she lurched forward, down a pair of steps and toward the driveway.

"That's a theory," El said, following her, "but I wouldn't bet on it."

On the other side of the house, as they trekked over snow toward the tree line, a gust of wind kicked up and seemed to cut right through El. He stopped to tuck his pant legs into his boots, and when he looked up Tess had turned her back to the trees and was waiting for him. She pulled the scarf away from her face to reveal a smile. "Hey!" she called. "It's gorgeous, isn't it?"

El gave himself a moment to take in the white expanse of field enclosed by towering green-and-white-speckled trees, their branches loaded with powdery snow. He jogged to catch up with Tess. When he reached her, he put his arm over her shoulder and pulled her close. She felt solid in his grasp, her body slim but muscular, and they continued trekking together through the snow toward the trees.

El's marriage had been a disaster, but as he walked through the cold and wind with his arm around Tess, his thoughts returned to the good early days, when he had been in love with his wife, when they used to take long walks and talk about their future. El hadn't had a loving thought about his wife in so long the memory left him feeling first disoriented and then sad. She had turned both his children against him. She had cost him a fortune in lawyer's fees. She'd wound up with the house and most of his retirement fund, so that now he'd never be able to retire comfortably. He was distant from his children, money was tight, and he'd be working in sales until he got too old to do it anymore. After that, he didn't know what would happen to him.

"Look," Tess said. She pointed to a gap in the trees.

"Trailhead." El squeezed Tess's shoulder and then let her loose. In the last several years, he had trained himself, with the help of a therapist, not to think much about his wife. There had been a point, before he started seeing a counselor, when he'd been so eaten up with bitterness he'd found himself thinking about murder and suicide, about killing his wife and his children and then himself. That he could even entertain such thoughts had frightened him into counseling. His therapist put him on medication for a couple of years, and that had helped—and now he lived an essentially solitary life that revolved around work. When he met people, it was through work. When he did anything social, it was through work. He had a distant, formal relationship with his children, and though he would have loved something more intimate, he didn't know how to make it happen. He hadn't spoken to his ex since the last time they'd met in a lawyer's office, at least six years earlier.

Once they were in the woods and out of the wind, it turned out Tess was right, and it was noticeably warmer. Tess leaned back against a boulder and undid her scarf, which she had wound around her neck and face. "Isn't it great to be out in this?" she said. "I love Manhattan, but, wow . . ." She gestured to the snow-covered trees and the scattering of rocks and boulders all around them. "I'd forgotten how beautiful."

El crouched in front of her and wrapped his arms around his knees. "But it's still cold," he said, "really cold."

"This world . . . ," Tess said, and she turned to look out through the trees, toward what appeared to be a meadow, some forty, fifty feet in front of them, at the bottom of a hill.

El pulled himself upright, embraced Tess, and kissed her. Tess seemed surprised at first, but then she put her arms around him and kissed him back.

"This is crazy," El said. "Don't you think?"

"What is?"

"Us," El said. "This." When Tess didn't answer, he said, "Is it just me?"

Tess watched El for a moment, her eyes on his eyes, and then she kissed him again. "It's all crazy," she said. She reached for his hand and pulled him along.

El followed Tess on the trail, which curved around one boulder that was several feet high, and then between a pair of boulders that formed a narrow corridor and opened onto a steep downhill slope to the meadow. When the wind stopped for a moment, the woods grew suddenly quiet. El let go of Tess's hand, possessed suddenly of an urge to touch the ragged surface of one of the boulders. As Tess continued down the hill, he took off one glove and pressed the palm of his hand to the rock. It was cold and solid. What else did he expect? Still, he held his hand against the stone and pushed his fingertips into the gritty surface. How long, he wondered, had this boulder been here, unmoved and unmoving? A few hundred thousand years? Millions? He rummaged around in his memory of geography classes and came up with an image of mountainous glaciers slowly retreating, gouging holes in the earth and leaving huge boulders scattered like pebbles.

Tess waved from the bottom of the hill. "Come look at this," she called. "It's lovely."

Before El reached Tess, midway down the hill, it occurred to him the meadow wasn't a meadow. It was too big, and there was something about the way the trees on the far side, now that he could see across . . . the trees all descended to the open space. It reminded him of his visits to the ocean in Oregon, the way the mountains descended to the sea. There was a space of perhaps two or three seconds between the moment it first dawned on him there was something odd about this meadow and the moment he realized it wasn't a meadow at all, but a pond, a large pond surrounded by woods—and in those two or three seconds, Tess stepped out onto the ice and her feet slid out from under her.

El yelled "Wait!" and started to jog down the hill. He had only taken a couple of steps when he tripped on something, a rock or an exposed root. To keep his balance, he reached for a tree and slammed sideways into it, and then lost his balance anyway and tumbled and rolled for several feet before finally coming to a stop. Through all this, he was keenly aware of the bulk of his body: it felt like a great weight, utterly beyond his control, radically different from the body of his youth, the one he could hurl about on the basketball court so athletically. He didn't know what shocked him more, the fall or that sense of his body as lumbering, uncontrollable bulk.

"It's all ice," Tess said. She had pulled herself to her feet and was looking up the hill. "Are you okay?" she asked. "You're bleeding."

"It's a pond," El called back to her. He wiped blood from the side of his face. First he thought he must have gotten scraped up when he hit the tree; then he realized there was too much blood, and he must have gashed himself somewhere.

"You think?" Tess said. She was crouched and looking at the ice under her feet, her arms spread for balance. "Guess so," she said.

A gust of wind came up and sent a spiral of snow across the pond as Tess took a careful step toward the shore and most of her body disappeared under the ice. El didn't hear anything crack. There was no sound at all. One moment Tess was upright on the ice and the next she was submerged to her shoulders.

Tess said "Oh," and then "Lord," and looked up at El as if she were embarrassed.

At the bottom of the hill, El got down on his knees and worked to extricate a long branch from a pile of icy brush. The gloves were interfering with his grip and so he pulled them off and tossed them onto the ice. Tess had said only those two words—"Oh" and "Lord"—and then she had gone silent as she struggled to pull herself out of the water, pushing her body forward. She appeared to be trying to walk, and slipping with each step. Her body lurched upright and then fell forward three times in quick succession, and then she stopped, her eyes open in a frightened glare, staring up the hill. She seemed to be conscious and aware. She was breathing hard, but she wasn't moving or speaking.

When El, at last, was able to pull the branch free, he lay down on his belly and extended it to Tess. The ice was cracked and shattered now all the way to the shoreline, and he could see that the dropoff was steep. Tess was only ten feet in front of him and the water was up to her breasts. "Take it," he yelled. Tess clutched her heart with one hand and looked at the branch as if she couldn't quite make out what it was or what to do with it. Her free arm rested easily on a heavy chunk of ice pressed up against her chest. "Take it," El repeated. "I'll pull you out. Grab hold of it."

Tess looked at El and then at the shore, and then she lunged at the branch, reaching for it with both hands. For a second she managed to grab hold of it. One moment her arms were wrapped around the branch, her whole body leaning over it—and the next moment she was gone, disappeared under the water.

El shouted her name and rose to his knees. An instant passed then that felt more like several minutes. First, he explored his options. He could try to run and get help—but that would be the equivalent of leaving her to die. He might try lying to himself, he might try rationalizing—but he knew if he left her there, the only point in returning would be to retrieve her body. Or he could go in after her. He'd have to submerge himself in the water, pull her out, and then carry her up the steep hill, across the long field, and back to the house. He figured the chances of succeeding were small. But maybe. Maybe he could do it. There was at least a chance.

Still, kneeling at the edge of the water he hesitated. His thoughts flew in a heartbeat first to his ex-wife, whom he saw in his mind for a moment vividly, her expression tender and concerned, and then to his children—and in a flash of memory he recalled his daughter falling from her bike, her legs and face scraped and bleeding, and how desperately she'd wrapped her arms around his neck as he carried her home. Both these images came to him in the instant's hesitation before he stepped into the freezing water.

The shock was stunning. It hit him like a body blow, as if he'd been slammed into a wall. After his first step he was in up to his waist, and the next step he was under water, struggling to make his brain work, commanding his feet to feel for the bottom, his arms to search for Tess. Then, a heartbeat later, there was no thought at all, only a panicked, urgent thrashing until he found Tess and pulled her to the surface choking and spitting. Her body seemed impossibly heavy, as did his own, the two of them weighed down by thick layers of soaked clothes. They were surrounded by chunks of ice and slushy water, and El had come up facing the opposite shore, so that what he saw in front of him was a wide expanse of pristine snow surrounded by trees. He leaned back, his arms around Tess's waist, and slipped and fell with his first attempt to take a backward step toward the shore. As he went under, his hip smacked into something hard and unmoving, and the impact was dull and sharp simultaneously—a dull thud and a sharp shock of heat shooting up his spine. When he found his footing again and came up out of the water, he was facing the shore, his arms still fast around Tess's waist.

They were close to solid ground now, only a few steps, only a few more feet—and El wasn't at all sure he could do it. His arms and legs felt stuck, unmovable, his arms wrapped around Tess as she continued to cough and spit while laboring to breathe, his legs planted under the water. With a grunt he gathered all his strength and surged forward, pushing Tess out in front of him, heaving her toward land, and then he was under the water again, his feet slipping out from under him, and when he broke the surface for the second time, he saw Tess clawing her way out of the pond, pulling herself to the shore. With what strength he had remaining, he flung his body toward her, pushing through chunks of ice that pummeled his chest and legs, until he was finally beside her, and he managed to pull both himself and Tess all the way out of the water before collapsing onto his back and breathing hard while he waited for his heart to quit its terrible pounding, to slow down enough that he could manage something more than his own hard breathing.

Though his body felt exhausted beyond functioning, his mind apparently was still working methodically. He entertained a dim hope that someone might have seen them struggling in the water. They were, after all, nearby a small American city: they weren't in the middle of the wilderness somewhere. Perhaps someone in a house on the other side of the pond, some kids out playing in the snow—perhaps someone saw them and was at that moment on the phone, dialing 911. Then, if they could hold on, others soon would be hurrying down the hill to take them away in ambulances—and all would be well. Maybe. El entertained these comforting thoughts until his heart stopped raging in his chest and he was able to turn over onto his side, where he found Tess, still on her back, breathing a little easier, looking up into the trees as if she saw something interesting there.

"Tess," he said, his voice raw. "Tess. Can you hear me?"

Tess nodded and turned her head to look at him. "I can't move," she whispered. Then her lips moved again, as if she might have thought she was speaking, but all that came out was a whisper of breath.

"Our clothes," he said. "They're weighing us down."

Tess looked back at him, but made no effort to speak.

"Okay," El said, with no idea what he meant. He struggled and managed to get himself sitting upright. His arms and legs felt as though they weighed tons, and it took him forever, fumbling with numb fingers, to get the zipper of his jacket down. By the time he had managed to get out of his coat and unwrap his tangled scarf from around his neck, he was exhausted again. He waited a moment and listened, his sodden jacket and scarf already beginning to freeze where they lay beside him in the snow. He had hoped to hear the sound of an engine in the distance, or the sound of boots trudging through the snow, or, best of all, maybe voices, voices calling for them.

But he heard nothing of the kind. Snow had started to come down harder, and the wind blew constantly. All he heard was the soft whisper of snowfall in the woods, and wind soughing through trees.

His first plan had been to carry Tess up the hill and back to the house—but that was impossible, and he understood that now with certainty. He could barely move himself, let alone carry Tess. He considered trying to get Tess out of her wet clothes, which he could see were already stiffening as ice crystals formed on the outer layers near her neck and wrists. He couldn't figure which would be better for her, to leave her packed inside wet, icy clothes, or to leave her further exposed to the wind and cold with them off. While he tried to consider that question, he noticed his thoughts had started to turn sluggish, and that frightened him into moving.

"I'm going," he said, meaning he was going to get help. He pulled himself to his feet and looked up the hill, which seemed to him now mountainously steep. He turned back one more time to Tess, stretched out on her back in a bright red jacket and green scarf, her hair stiff with ice, a light layer of bright new snow untouched around her. He thought to shout something reassuring to her, but he couldn't come up with words, and he realized he was at least a little dazed now and his mind wasn't functioning entirely right—and again that realization provided the surge of energy he needed to push himself forward and up the hill.

His exhaustion was overwhelming, like nothing he'd ever felt before. Even in his days playing basketball, when he'd sprint from one end of the court to the other at full speed until his legs finally gave out, when he'd fly up and down the stadium stairs, or work the weight machines until his arms were rubbery—none of it was anything like the exhaustion he felt climbing that hill. Each step required all his remaining will. Every time he fell, he tried to fall forward, so that when he got up again, which he did, over and over, he'd made a little progress, moving himself farther along— and in that manner he made it to the top of the hill, where he could see through the trees to the open field behind their B and B. In another fifty feet, he'd be out of the woods—and even if he couldn't make it all the way across the field, he still might be seen by someone, by the old woman who owned the house, by kids out playing, by a car passing on the road. If he could make it out of the woods, he told himself, his chances were better, and if he could make it all the way to the house, he might yet still save himself and maybe Tess, maybe Tess also could be saved.

With those thoughts rattling around in his head, he stumbled forward, pushing himself one step at a time, and not until he reached the pair of boulders that formed a narrow corridor, did he allow himself to fall to his knees and rest a moment . . . just a moment, out of the stabbing wind, within the protection of the two ancient rocks, the one he had touched with wonder a million years ago, when the earth was still young and much was possible; when Tess, a woman who had appeared out of nowhere in his life and with whom he had been peacefully cuddled in the warmth of a down comforter the night before; when Tess, who was beautiful and smart and funny; when Tess was a dozen feet in front of him and ambling down a hill toward the pond that they both thought then was a meadow. He was at ease there, between those rocks, and suddenly, overpoweringly sleepy. When he thought about the intense desire to sleep that was overcoming him, and when he realized at the same moment he was no longer kneeling, but rather he was stretched out on his belly between the boulders, he had another, brief, panicky moment. He knew he had to pull himself up to his feet, he had to get up and keep moving, and he pushed his mind back to the images that had come to him in the moment before he stepped into the water, in that moment when he made his choice to go in after Tess. He remembered his children and his wife, and his daughter's arms around his neck as he carried her home.

One more time, then, he struggled to pull himself to his feet, and when his body wouldn't move, he struggled harder, he struggled with all he had in him; and at the moment when he was about to give up, when he was on the verge of resigning himself to sleep, at that moment, suddenly, miraculously, he was fine. He was saved, both he and Tess. Together they walked away from the cold, out of the woods and over the surface of the pond. All around them, pristine snow gathered. When the wind blew, it danced in circles and sailed off into the stands of surrounding trees. They had both taken off their clothes to free themselves of the sopping, burdensome weight, and they walked easily over the ice, sure-footedly, side by side, leaving a trail of mist behind them, falling off them like smoke. The mist coming off Tess was white and wispy, while the mist off El was thick and swirling and tinted red. He saw himself then as if from above, a big man, bulky, walking beside Tess on the pond, leaving a cloud of red mist behind him, as if his body were casting off heat and leaving behind a trail of flame. He continued watching calmly, the bodies beneath him on the ice growing smaller and smaller as he rose higher, until they were merely points of light, and then they were nothing at all.

EDWARD FALCO is the author of three other story collections, three novels, and nine plays, in addition to a collection of short shorts, a hypertext novel, hypertext short fictions, and several online works of new media writing. He has also published many poems, essays, and book reviews. Among his awards are an NEA fiction fellowship, the Emily Clark Balch Prize in Fiction, the Robert Penn Warren Prize in Poetry, three Virginia Commission for the Arts fellowships, and the Hampden-Sydney Playwriting Award. He is currently a professor of English at Virginia Tech, where he directs the MFA Program in Creative Writing.